Dead Man Who Walks Away

The entrance to Massacre Ground

Dead Man Who Walks Away

Part I

The Peralta / The Massacre

Herbert Dean Ely

MILFORD HOUSE

an imprint of Sunbury Press, Inc.
Mechanicsburg, PA USA

MILFORD HOUSE

an imprint of Sunbury Press, Inc.
Mechanicsburg, PA USA

For information about special discounts for bulk purchases, please contact Sunbury Press Orders Dept. at (855) 338-8359 or orders@sunburypress.com.

To request one of our authors for speaking engagements or book signings, please contact Sunbury Press Publicity Dept. at publicity@sunburypress.com.

FIRST MILFORD HOUSE PRESS EDITION: August 2023

Set in Adobe Garamond Pro | Interior design by Crystal Devine | Cover by Lawrence Knorr | Edited by Taylor Berger-Knorr.

Publisher's Cataloging-in-Publication Data
Names: Ely, Herbert Dean, author.
Title: Dead man who walks away part I / the peralta / the massacre / Herbert Dean Ely.
Description: First trade paperback edition. | Mechanicsburg, PA : Milford House Press, 2023.
Summary: *Dead Man Who Walks Away* is based upon physical locations and events, all of which were possible during that early period of the Southwest. The Lost Dutchman Mine existed but, as this account shows, not the way perceived in past accounts.
Identifiers: ISBN : 979-8-88819-108-8 (paperback) | ISBN : 979-8-88819-109-5 (ePub).
Subjects: FICTION / Historical / General | FICTION / Fairy Tales, Folk Tales, Legends & Mythology.

Product of the United States of America
0 1 1 2 3 5 8 13 21 34 55

For the Love of Books!

To my lovely wife, JoAnn, who has suffered through the long period of my research and efforts to get this book right; my sons – Jon, Jeff, and daughter Jacqui; grandkids – Brian, Chris, Lauren, Katie, Megan, Bradley, Jake, and Dana—all who were probably wondering "Is he serious?"

Acknowledgments

My thanks go out to my longtime friend, Mr. Jim Davia, who walked, climbed, and jumped the rocks and ravines, dodged rattlesnakes, and searched the desert locales of this story to find and visit the "Lost Dutchman Mine." The origin of the gold of the Lost Dutchman Mine is the subject of this legend. Many thanks! For the use of the Spanish version of his name, Diego DaVia, muchas gracias!

My thanks to my friend Mr. Bruce Johnson, retired educator from Illinois, for his time and interest in "Dead Man Who Walks Away." His effort is especially appreciated for having accompanied me to Massacre Ground as well as other pertinent locales important to this story.

Preface

Peralta!

Even now the name Peralta stirs the imagination of people in the southwestern deserts of Arizona and New Mexico. The aristocratic Peralta family of northern Sonora, who ruled their empire of mining, cattle, and lumber from Sonora to California, left their mark on the early history of the Southwest. But then, and even to this day, the only item of genuine interest to Sonoran Desert dwellers was the mining. Gold mining. For a hundred years after the Jesuit and Franciscan padres forced Indian laborers to work their mines, the Peraltas continued to reap the gold from the land of the Yavapai and Apache tribes. Until driven out by the Yavapai, the Peralta family had been the controlling economic force in what is now Arizona.

Then, during the period of 1848 to 1854, after the Mexican-American war, events led to the Gadsden Purchase of what is now the southern portion of the state of Arizona. Prior to that purchase, Don Miguel Peralta, with financing and military support from Antonio de Lopez de Santa Anna, President of Mexico, embarked on a large expedition to the old mines in what is now Arizona to retrieve as much gold as possible before that Gadsden Purchase became fact. That endeavor was *almost* successful.

Realizing that the Yavapai and their allies, the Apache, were about to attack in retaliation for their mistreatment and lack of due respect, the Peralta expedition made a desperate run to save their lives and their gold. The Yavapai and the Apache trapped them just northwest of Superstition

Mountain in a box canyon now known as "Massacre Ground." The Peralta miners and their Mexican cavalry all died, save one, Lieutenant Diego DaVia. Somehow, a day or so after the slaughter, an injured Lieutenant Diego DaVia pulled himself from under his dead horse and, with his mind reeling from the horror of what he had just survived, walked away.

High on a hillside overlooking the tragic scene, the great Yavapai warrior O hi Cama and a young shaman of the Apache watched him make his way out of that canyon. They marveled at his survival and feared his medicine. O hi Cama remembered him well as the very capable and brave soldier. He referred to Lieutenant DaVia as "Dead Man Who Walks Away." Thus, would Lieutenant Diego DaVia be forever known among the Yavapai and Apache and avoided by those warriors who knew his story. Lieutenant Diego DaVia became "Dead Man Who Walks Away."

This is the story of the Peralta and the massacre. Part II is the story of the survivor and the Dutchman's gold.

Prologue

In what is now the state of Arizona there exists a box canyon. The canyon's entrance faces the setting sun, sloping somewhat gently eastward and upward until it reaches the far wall. Now strewn with boulders and cacti and overgrown with bristly brush, it hides the grisly beginning of a golden legend.

Bones of horses, mules, and of men at one time littered the floor of this bleak, unforgiving canyon. Among the bleaching bones, here and there, filling the small crevices in the rocks or making small piles of glittering dust on the granite floor . . . gold! Some of it had washed away. Some of it had merely settled into the dirt and gravel. Some had been picked up by prospectors or wandering drifters. Each one thought that he had just found "El Dorado," the fabulous wealth each of them dreamed would change their lives.

Unfortunately, what they had found was merely float gold—gold that was there, not by nature, but dropped there at the same time as the living bones had dropped there, in the canyon that is now called "Massacre Ground."

With no written language of their own, the story was told only by the old ones of the Yavapai and the Apache.

The breeze plays among the thorny branches of the canyon's brush. Mesquite, ocotillo, saguaro, and many other forms of cacti abound. During the day, the blinding white-hot sun of summer bakes every inch of the canyon floor too hot for man or beast to walk upon. Yet now and then, usually during the cool winter months, a wanderer ventures into the canyon. Having taken his fill of its stark desert beauty, the wanderer begins to feel uneasy and hurries to find a trail out of the canyon. Something in this canyon, unseen, perhaps the spirits of those who cannot leave, warn him of danger. Wisely, without turning back, he departs, leaving the canyon to only the sun and the breeze and the shadows of the past.

The year was 1848.

The place was Mexico City, Mexico.

In the office of El Presidente Antonio de Lopez de Santa Anna, two men met behind closed doors. El presidente had agreed to meet with Don Miguel Peralta, a prominent citizen of the province of Sonora.

Don Peralta was somewhat apprehensive about this meeting, in spite of the fact that he himself had requested it. After all, El Presidente Santa Anna was not always in the best frame of mind. Santa Anna had the power to back up whatever whim he sought to pursue, good or bad, fair or unfair. Don Peralta was sure of only one thing concerning el presidente: greed was a primary motive in anything Santa Anna did. Therefore, he gathered himself, smiled, and greeted Santa Anna warmly. To his relief, el presidente returned his greeting in kind.

"Don Peralta, please forgive me for not providing you with this audience earlier. Matters of state you know," said el presidente.

"Please, Excellency, forgive my impatience in seeking this audience. My own urgency of purpose dominated my thoughts. These are difficult times," responded Don Peralta.

"Times are changing for all of us. I, above all, realize this. Having been in and out of power in Mexico several times I, more so than most, have lived with this fact," jokingly asserted Santa Anna. "Yet, as your presidente, I feel not obligated but privileged to honor your request. Knowing your family's history of loyal service to Mexico, I am sure your motive for requesting this visit is worthwhile."

"With your participation, I believe we both will profit from it, Excellency," assured Don Peralta.

"You have my attention," said Santa Anna.

"I will not waste your time relating details of events of which you are doubtless already aware, Excellency; but I must bring some facts to your attention," stated Don Peralta.

"I would appreciate such clarification," replied el presidente.

"Gold mining has taken place in the mountains of northern Sonora for nearly two centuries," continued Don Peralta. "The church's missions along 'El Camino Real' found gold in abundance. This gold was transported across Sonora, Chihuahua, and eventually shipped to the Spanish king in galleons. The Jesuits, with the blessing of the king of Spain, were given control of the mining of this gold. This contract with the Jesuits was not given out of the goodness of the king's heart. The king of Spain demanded twenty percent of the gold taken from these mines."

"The king of Spain was no fool," spoke el presidente approvingly.

"That lucrative arrangement lasted until the 1740s. Reports were received that the Jesuit order was caching gold in various mines to avoid paying the king his twenty percent. The king of Spain, in anger, cancelled the agreement with the Jesuits and ordered the mining rights be divided among private interests including the Franciscan order of the church. Of course, each party was mindful of the king's twenty percent fee. I am pleased to say that, in later years, my ancestors were allowed to pursue mining interests in Sonora and even lumber and ranching in California, which continues to this day," related Don Peralta.

"But, as you also know, the Jesuits had used primarily Indian labor to work these mines, willingly or even under the whip, as it were. That method of operation was continued under the new management as well. Over the ensuing decades, various Indian tribes revolted, and these tribes have since made mining in the North extremely dangerous. The attacks have made it too dangerous for small mining operations to continue and so they were discontinued by my family some time ago. Of this you are already aware. However, I would not make the suggestions I intend to make without speaking of this risk to you. My personal honor and the honor of my family would not allow me to deceive you, Excellency," stated Don Peralta.

"The honor of the Peralta family is well known to me, Don Miguel. Please continue," said el presidente.

"The United States, now in possession of California, has greatly curtailed the profitability of my family's ventures in California, but we know there is much gold remaining in our abandoned mines in northern Sonora," continued Don Peralta.

"You have my interest, Don Peralta. Please proceed," said Santa Anna.

"The amount of gold remaining in northern Sonora is still immense. However, the Indian menace precludes any small expedition. Also, in addition to that danger, a more pressing situation necessitates serious consideration: North American expansion. I am sure you will agree such expansion on their part is inevitable. Whatever form it takes, it will forever remove any chance we might have to access that gold," warned Don Peralta. At that, el presidente raised his hand to interrupt the conversation.

"Excuse me, Don Peralta," said Santa Anna, rising and making his way to and opening the door of his office. "Sentry, be sure I am not disturbed until further ordered."

Returning to his desk, he offered Don Miguel some wine and said, "Please go on, Don Peralta. The subject of gold has always piqued my interest."

"As I was saying, Excellency, North American expansion is coming to that area just as surely as we are now speaking of it. We still have time, a few short years perhaps, to extricate that gold for Mexico and for ourselves," spoke the don. Don Miguel paused a moment to let his words have their effect. Then, leaning forward and looking el presidente eye to eye, he said, "My plan is this, presidente mio: I propose we mount a large, well-equipped expedition to mine as much remaining gold as possible from northern Sonora before the Americans arrive."

"You intrigue me, Don Peralta. But, as el Presidente of Mexico, I cannot personally join such an expedition. Therefore, I presume you are asking me to invest somehow in this highly dangerous venture. Am I correct?" asked Santa Anna.

"I will explain exactly what I propose," said Don Peralta. "Then, we will discuss possible investment.

"The Sombrero Mines, begun by the old Spanish and operated by my family north of the Rio Salado, consist of perhaps twenty-five to fifty rich locations. They are located in fairly close proximity to each other within a circle two to three miles in diameter. We must have enough men to work them and to defend them. I humbly suggest that we mount a force of two hundred men, with two hundred mules, and work those mines for no more than two years. At that time, we will transport the gold in mule packs back to sovereign Mexican soil . . . and to us. I am sure we can load two hundred mules with one hundred pounds of gold each. Twenty thousand pounds of gold for Mexico and for us," promised Don Peralta, never lowering his eyes from those of el presidente.

"Don Peralta, you certainly are ambitious. Why are you suggesting transporting the gold by mule rather than in wagons? It seems that you do not intend to smelt it into bars. Why?" questioned Santa Anna.

"There is nothing even remotely resembling a road in that area. Heavy wagons loaded with gold bullion will never make it. I intend to break the gold from the quartz using the old Spanish arrastras and pack the dust and nuggets in bags, then transport the processed gold by mule back," returned the don.

"Well thought out, Don Miguel," said Santa Anna. "But I trust that I am not being asked to provide the entire investment in order to satisfy your ambition," stated Santa Anna flatly.

"I am prepared to invest all of my family's assets. I am hoping for a similar sum from you personally, or as a grant from the Mexican government. The cost of outfitting, mining equipment, livestock, payment of subsistence for the men, and unforeseen expense is no small amount, but the return greatly justifies the expense," assured Don Peralta.

The president of Mexico sat silent for a time. Don Miguel, not wishing to interrupt Santa Anna's thoughts, patiently awaited his response. El Presidente Santa Anna's response was slow in coming, but finally he said in a very low tone, "You have come at a most advantageous time, Don Miguel. I will confide in you information that you will never divulge under penalty of death. Do you understand and agree?" asked el presidente.

"Yes," agreed Don Peralta.

"I am, at the present moment, involved in very preliminary negotiations with the United States to allow their purchase of an area south of the Rio Salado and Rio Gila. I have been approached by North American business representatives. These men will be laying the foundation for later official negotiations. Officially, the United States government has not been approached, but they will be. Evidently, the North Americans overlooked this area at the end of our recent war. It seems they need to use it as a route to San Diego and southern California. This will cost them much. The negotiations will take a few years, mostly because communications take so long. Actually, having been recently forced to cede so much of Mexico's territory to them already, I see no reason not to 'hold their feet to the fire' for a while. However, when we come to terms—and we will—I have the ability to delay acceptance until after we complete such a venture as you describe," said Santa Anna. "Without doubt, after the Americans take possession of this area, your mining rights as a Mexican citizen on United States soil will be worthless."

"I am very much aware of that fact, Excellency. I must admit that I foresaw these changes coming; and, somehow, I felt that time was short. With the information you have just entrusted to me, I did not realize how very short!" exclaimed Don Peralta. "No one must know of this until our expedition has returned. I will keep our destination and motive completely secret."

El Presidente, his decision made, stood and outlined his thoughts.

"Our preliminary agreement is this: you will not have to invest all of your family treasure, Don Peralta. The fact that you were willing to do so is most reassuring to me. Because this is definitely in Mexico's interest, my government will invest a substantial amount. My own funds are somewhat limited. Based upon profitability, my personal share of the profits will be at least that of the former king of Spain—twenty percent of the gross. You will take fifty of my military—cavalry—to accompany you and protect both our interests. If you do not agree, this project is terminated. Do you agree, Don Peralta?" asked el presidente.

"I most heartily agree, presidente mio," vowed Don Peralta.

Arizpe, Sonora, Mexico

There was much to do. Even though Don Peralta had been planning this attempt to retrieve what he felt was rightfully his family's gold from the mines in northern Sonora, his preliminary efforts were as yet simply not enough. Stockpiling of tools and equipment had been going forward for months. He needed yet to arrange for many mules, horses, and—most critically—men. Thanks to El Presidente Santa Anna, weapons and supplies were, at last, at his disposal. But trustworthy men were hard to find.

Returning soldiers from the recently lost war with the United States had found very little work to support them. Many had turned to thievery and worse to keep themselves and their families alive. The term "banditos" had become the description of a newly resurrected career field. Thus, some were even willing to join a "mystery" expedition, justified only by the word of Don Miguel Peralta. Still, the selection process took time.

Don Miguel Peralta had three sons: Pedro, Manuel, and Ramón. He was very proud of his sons. However, he could not take all three on this journey. For one thing, someone had to stay back and direct the various Peralta enterprises. Pedro was married and had children. Ramón was young; and this excursion was not going to be a picnic. Manuel was hardly ever home, was single—a bit of a rogue, showing little sense of responsibility. All his life, he had been a rebel. However, Manuel was also not a man to be dissuaded from whatever he set his mind to do. This job would require such a man.

Don Miguel had intended to choose Manuel anyway. The other two must remain behind.

Manuel Peralta, young, dashing, full of adventure, was the kind of man who would never allow himself to be left behind. Slim, yet muscular, with a trimmed dark mustache and piercing eyes, he cut an aristocratic figure.

Manuel Peralta had joined the Mexican army in time for the war's end. He participated in one battle only but distinguished himself well. In spite of the attention shown to the young officer by the ladies, he reluctantly made his way home to his family's rancheria in Arizpe, Sonora. After many days' ride, he halted his horse on a hill that offered a full view of the rancheria below.

The sight that greeted Manuel Peralta as he observed the rancheria stunned him. In the late afternoon light, standing in the stirrups, overlooking the rancheria, he saw before him what amounted to an armed camp. At first, he thought some military force had taken over. He was greatly relieved upon seeing his father striding about giving orders. Assured by this that all was well, he charged into the rancheria at full gallop to make his usual grand entrance. It was a good thing that his father was there, because a few of the expedition's young recruits had already drawn their weapons at his approach. It required a sharp command from his father to calm the situation. Through the swirling dust, Don Peralta heard the familiar hearty laugh of his caballero son.

"Is this any way to greet a soldier returning from a war?" laughed Manuel to his father. "Another army ready to shoot me?"

Don Miguel could never resist laughing at the words of his happy-go-lucky son. "If I had wanted you shot, I'd have done it myself long ago. What delayed your return so long? Or is a young woman's enraged father about to arrive also?"

"Calm your fears, Father. If that were the case, I'd have outrun him long ago," said Manuel, as father and son embraced. "Tell me what is going on around here. But tell me while I am eating. I need food!"

Manuel's mother was already running to greet her son.

"Mamacita, your son is home! Greet him and then feed him," said Don Miguel.

Manuel hugged his mother tightly until she backed away and said, "Did no one bother to feed you in that stupid army? Look at you. You are skin stretched over bones. Wash up and come inside. I will soon fatten you up."

Manuel did not fatten up as soon as promised, but it was not his mother's fault. He feasted until he could not move. Little did he know, in his future, such feasts would be few and spaced far apart.

"Father, what is going on? What are we up to?" he asked.

"We? What makes you think you are involved?" Don Miguel replied.

"I see uniformed men, guns, mules, horses, and supply packs piled all over the place, and you barking out orders to these men. Well, the only thing missing is . . . me. Of course, I'm involved. Where are we going? What are we doing? And when are we doing it? Frankly, it looks like I almost missed the departure," asserted Manuel.

For just a moment only silence was heard in the room. Then, from the doorway, came the rustling of skirts.

"Your mother has left the room for a moment, so I will speak," quietly said the don. "The expedition is dangerous, full of hardships. We will be gone for at least two years. Some or all of us could be killed. And special information just for you . . . there will be no women involved."

"Going after the abandoned Sombrero Mines gold, huh?" guessed Manuel. The Sombrero Mines were named for the rocky formation nearby that made the mountain range look as though it were wearing a sombrero.

Sombrero Mountain

"That is supposed to be a secret. Be quiet," ordered the don. "How did you know this?"

"You've been drooling over that idea for years," answered Manuel. "I have often wondered when you would get around to it."

"Nonetheless, no one here knows but I and now you. No one. They enjoy the mystery of it right now; but if word got out, many would desert. And a very powerful man would be out looking for me. Do you understand? *Comprende?*" ordered Don Miguel.

"What about Pedro and Ramón, Father?" asked Manuel.

"They are content at the moment. They are remaining here to operate our other enterprises. This is a decision I have just made. Your enthusiasm has forced that decision. I pray it does not get you killed," replied the don. "We leave for el sombrero within the week."

"Good. I was afraid I would not have time to shed this damn uniform!" exclaimed the newly created civilian.

Manuel's laugh lasted only a very short moment, until the darkly sobering look on his father's face showed him how serious were his father's words.

Shortly after his decision to take Manuel to the Sombrero Mines, Don Miguel met with his sons Pedro and Ramón. Both understood the enormity of such a quest. Both realized the reasons why they must remain behind. Both were supportive of the don and their brother Manuel. This did not make them any happier about not being selected, but both were aware of, and accepted, the responsibility placed upon them.

For the Peraltas, all their attention was now focused northward.

3

Arizpe, Sonora, a small village, nestled among high mountains along the Rio Sonora. From there, early in the morning, on a bright, early autumn day, the expedition set out. Despite the large number of men and their equipment, and because of the remoteness of the rugged mountains surrounding the little valley, no one marked the expedition's departure. There was no fanfare. After quiet goodbyes and long hugs from some local friends and family members, the long column of mounted men and their mules silently moved out toward the north.

The men still did not know where their final destination would be; but they knew, from the tools they were bringing, that mining would be their work. Some were excited about the prospect. Others were having second thoughts about having joined this mission. The volume of supplies indicated that they would be gone a long time. The materials aboard the pack train surely meant that a great quantity of something would be brought back to Sonora. Eight wagons containing tools, a great quantity of dry food, weapons, and ammunition, plus a chuck wagon, brought up the rear of the column. Don Peralta, aware of the difficulties involved in wagon travel over rough, virgin terrain, preferred to limit them to light vehicles with narrow wheelbases. However, the military command insisted upon their heavy, army-issue wagons. The military supplied all of these. Don Miguel warned Manuel that these wagons might not make it. Plans must be made to react to that possibility. Without being told, the soldiers suspected that the expedition sought great wealth. Seduced by the mystery, they turned their faces northward.

The civilian men, only recently made aware of the contingent of military cavalry to accompany them, began to draw their own conclusions about this mission. They began to realize that it would be dangerous, but realized also that there would be no turning back.

Don Miguel Peralta, by no means a young man, still presented an imposing figure as he led the procession. Astride his horse, with rigid posture, he was the very image of the Spanish aristocrat. The short waistcoat and the stiff, wide-brimmed black hat, coupled with the slightly graying hair and mustache, portrayed him to be every inch the Spanish nobleman. The saber of a cavalry officer at his side, he rode in full command. Manuel Peralta, the young son, rode proudly at his father's side. Although his clothing was more the uniform of the vaquero, he had managed to keep his own cavalry saber and wore it at his side.

They would have a long hard trek ahead of them. It was over three hundred trackless miles from Arizpe to the region of the Sombrero Mines. Their route would take them northward along the Rio Sonora, through high mountains on through open plains into the land of the Chiricahua Apache, the Rio San Pedro Valley. They would have to follow the Rio San Pedro as long as they could until they crossed the Rio Gila. They would have to proceed still farther northward, working their torturous way past the west end of the Superstition Mountain range, cross the Rio Salado, and then up the Rio Verde.

Most of this entire route, with the exception of the mountains near Arizpe, was unforgiving desert. The route after they left the Rio San Pedro, they would find, was extremely dry and dangerous. The Rio Verde would possibly offer some respite from the dry surroundings. The river normally flowed nearly all year long, providing water and lush, green vegetation along its banks. The adventurers would greatly relish the shade along the banks of the Rio Verde.

Eventually, the party would have to make its way up the occasionally dry canyon (now called Camp Creek) that worked its way northwestward from the Rio Verde to the area of the Sombrero Mines.

The expedition could look forward to at least a month's very difficult travel . . . if they were lucky.

However, as the expedition left the village of Arizpe, and the sun rose over the mountainous horizon, spirits were high. These were very tough men used to fighting adversity and calling it adventure. And this was certain to be an adventure. There was much laughter. Only the military personnel sent by El Presidente Santa Anna were quiet. Their military training would have them forego any spontaneous talking or laughing in their ranks, even if their superior officers allowed it.

Don Miguel Peralta sat on his horse as if he were, himself, a general leading his troops. His face showed a regal sense of pride in what he was now endeavoring to accomplish. With his son Manuel at his side, he felt he had a right to be proud.

Manuel Peralta felt the same pride in his father as to what he had accomplished thus far. He always had been proud of his father. From earliest childhood, Manuel tried to emulate him. But to actually be riding beside the don, on an adventure together . . . his heart swelled. All the boisterous, rash, reckless things he had done prior to his abbreviated service in the Mexican army had always been done to earn his father's respect.

And the word spread—northward. The Indians, Yaqui and Apache, knew the expedition had left Arizpe almost immediately. They knew not its mission nor its destination, but they knew it was pointed northward. The expedition's size and its northward heading were seen as a warning to Yaqui and Apache both. From every hilltop, their scouts marked the expedition's way over every mile of its long trek. For a time, the Indians along the way would be content just to know of the column's progress. None of the tribes was in any position to interfere with an armed force of two hundred-fifty men. They would watch and . . . wait.

From Arizpe, southward through the heartland of Mexico, to Mexico City, word of the expedition's departure went largely unnoticed. El Presidente Santa Anna preferred it that way. Therefore, that was the way it was.

The first few days after leaving Arizpe were largely uneventful. The spirits of the adventurers were high. They were still moving northward over a not-too-difficult trail, following the Rio Sonora, surrounded by mountains and hills. If they noticed the Indians in the distance marking their way, it caused them no great concern. After all, they were two hundred-fifty strong. Then again, these Indians were Yaquis, and the procession would be leaving the land of the Yaqui. A comparative short distance ahead, the procession would enter the land of the Apache, "Apacheria!" While the expedition kept moving away from them, the Yaquis would probably cause them no trouble. Apacheria could be another matter altogether. El capitán, Antonio Garces, commander of the military unit, placed scouts in front and behind the column.

Capitán Antonio Garces was a veteran officer, having served directly under the command of then-General Santa Anna. He was in his early thirties, unmarried, and dedicated to his duty. He took great pride in his execution of orders and accomplishment of his assigned mission. Because of this, he was well respected among his fellow officers. Capitán Garces rode at the head of the military column but occasionally advanced to Don Miguel's side. Both had apprehensions concerning the Indians, but they realized that an attack was not likely . . . not there. However, it was a good thing for the men to see that precautions were being taken.

Capitán Antonio Garces was every bit the career military officer. He was tall, just over six feet. He had the lean, lithe look of quickness about him. His dark eyes seemed to see beyond the range of vision of other men. He had the look of eagles as was once described. His subordinates preferred not to be the object of his gaze.

Manuel Peralta very soon began to respect Capitán Garces. Having just spent some time in the military himself, he understood Capitán Garces's motives. The responsibility to provide safety and security for this large force must weigh heavily upon him. Capitán Garces tolerated no laxness in his troops' conduct or attention. Even though no attack was expected, he kept his men at a high level of alert. He knew the priority given to this venture by el presidente and was determined that nothing would adversely affect it on his watch. Although conversations were few at first between them, Manuel began to like the man.

———

No major problems occurred in the first few days, but progress was extremely slow. The trail the men laughingly called a road became no more than a pathway. The horses and mules had no trouble traversing the narrow path, but the wagons immediately began to have trouble. The ruts and the narrow path between rocks and trees caused detours and wasted much time. The procession was making less than one mile per hour. Don Miguel Peralta had been correct in his assessment of the large, wide wagons. Unfortunately, he was stuck with them.

———

Five days into the trip, the formation camped outside the tiny village of Cananea. Here the men tried to rest, while Don Peralta and Manuel made some purchases in Cananea to replace many necessities. While in the village, Don Peralta made a courtesy call on the alcalde (mayor) of the village.

The office of the alcalde was on the second floor of the large white stucco building. The traditional walled courtyard and garden below made for a very pleasant respite to await the alcalde. Don Peralta did not have to wait long.

"Don Miguel Peralta! Welcome! It has been too long. Enter and refresh yourself," greeted the alcalde. To his aide, the alcalde ordered, "Bring wine for our honored guest."

Don Enrique Vasquez, alcalde of Cananea, once the robust cattle rancher of years past, had succumbed to the good life of his office. He had become a bit portly and sported a pot belly. But the fiery look in his eyes gave one the feeling that he could still do some really serious damage, if necessary.

"Thank you, Enrique, my old friend. It has, indeed, been a long time. I am honored to be so well received," Don Miguel said to Don Enrique Vasquez, alcalde of Cananea. "This fine wine—and this grand oak chair—is welcome indeed. It has been only five days since leaving Arizpe, but my bones swear to me that it has been five years."

"We knew you would be coming. I believe all northern Sonora knew it. A fine procession like yours cannot remain a secret for long in Sonora," said the alcalde. "The Yaquis have been talking of nothing else since you climbed into the saddle. It would please me greatly for you to tell me of your mission, but I know you too well to press the issue."

"Yes. Pressing the issue would accomplish nothing. But you have been my good friend for many years. Speaking of it to you, my friend, would please me very much. Your opinion would be welcome, also," assured Don Miguel.

"That is good to know, but I also know that my opinion would not change your mind once you have decided. And you have obviously already decided," said Don Enrique Vasquez, laughing.

"Ha! That is true, old friend," stated Don Miguel. "But I will gladly tell you what this trip is all about."

"I have known you for many years, Don Miguel. You are a very successful man and have become involved in many operations: mining, lumber, ranching. You hate farming. There is no reason to go north for lumber. Ranching . . . in Apacheria? No, it has to be mining. The gold that your family had to leave behind many years ago has been calling to you for years. You are at last on your way to get it. Tell me if I am wrong," said Don Enrique grinning.

"I cannot do that," agreed Don Miguel. "You know me too well. I hope that being my good friend does not eventually get you in trouble. Someday soon I may need such a friend."

"Should you need me, simply let me know," assured the alcalde.

"My son Manuel is my right arm on this venture, Enrique. He is now in your shops buying some supplies to replace what we have already wasted. I am forced to bring the large military wagons into a land that hates wagons. The gullies, arroyos, ravines, rocks . . . whatever else exists between here and el sombrero will eat those damn wagons," said Don Miguel through gritted teeth.

"Madre mia, you will spend more time fixing those wagons than mining gold," agreed Don Enrique.

"My friend, I wish you would pay an occasional visit to my family in Arizpe while I am away. My sons Pedro and Ramón are now in charge; but an older, wiser visitor for them, full of good advice, would ease my mind," said Don Miguel.

"I will make it my mission," promised the alcalde. "How long will you be gone?"

"I expect it will be over two years," said Don Miguel.

"I know that this venture to el sombrero is nearest to your heart now, Don Miguel; but there is now something else to think about—your rancheria and holdings in California," said Don Enrique.

"What do you mean, Enrique?" asked Don Miguel.

"We heard two days ago by messenger that much gold has been discovered in January of this year, at a place called Sutter's Mill in central California. A rush for gold has begun. People from all over the world will be heading for the gold fields . . . the Americans, most of all," said Don Enrique.

"My family's holdings will be in jeopardy due to encroachment by the Americans. Until now, we have had very few problems. Now, we will probably be under much more pressure. Land titles must be secured. Business and political relationships must be renewed and expanded. The Americans have not applied much pressure yet, but I know it will come. What can I do, Enrique? What do you suggest?" wondered Don Miguel.

"You can do nothing now," voiced the alcalde. "You are needed to lead this trek to the Sombrero Mines."

"You are right. I cannot leave for California. I must see that this expedition fulfills its mission," said Don Miguel. "I am committed."

"I don't think disaster will happen so soon," said the alcalde. "There may be time to do both."

"There is no choice for me right now," said Don Miguel. "I ask you this, Enrique: get word to Pedro and Ramón to send dispatches to our representatives in California. They must verify and secure the deeds to our properties in the American courts. I must return to my men. Manuel will need some help organizing the new supplies. Thank you, my friend."

"Farewell and Godspeed, Don Miguel," said the alcalde.

Don Miguel left the office of the alcalde with haste. He wished to be alone for a time. Manuel was fully capable of handling the new supplies. Don Miguel just needed to be alone for a while to gather his thoughts. This much he knew: he had absolutely no course but to continue to el sombrero. He alone knew where the various mines of el sombrero were to be found. Once mining was resumed, he would decide what to do, and not until.

5

The next morning, the procession moved northeastward from the village of Cananea and out onto the more open plain. The open desert countryside afforded them a better view of what was to come than had the close, wooded mountains. There was not much chance that they would see civilization of any consequence for some time to come. The plain, aside from some occasional rolling hills, looked dry and bleak. How fortunate that they had not begun this trek during the extreme heat of summer.

Thanks to the discipline of both the military and the control of Manuel and his own miner squad leaders, the procession moved in close formation as they proceeded across this open plain. To the unseen Yaqui Indians watching them, the expedition must have looked formidable indeed.

Don Miguel waved to Manuel to ride to his side.

"We have been slowed considerably by those mountains and those damn wagons," Don Miguel said to Manuel. "We need to make up for at least some of that delay on this open plain."

"I will give the orders," responded Manuel.

Manuel rode up and down the line of horses and mules exhorting the men to hurry, avoid any ravines, and to pick the line of travel offering the least obstruction.

"Capitán Garces, have your men pick up the pace. We need to make up for some of the time we have lost," voiced Manuel.

"I have already given the order, Manuel," said Capitán Garces. "But we cannot risk damage to the wagons. We will have to occasionally break from the rest of the column to do this."

"Yes, I know, Capitán," agreed Manuel. "But we cannot drift too far from each other. The danger here is small, but we must not seem to split our columns."

"I do not expect any kind of attack from the Yaquis, but I do not want to start any bad habits so soon into this march," said el capitán. "When we get into much wilder country, we must have a plan to work with these wagons better. I hope you are aware that these damn wagons were not my idea," stated el capitán.

"I know that, but lucky us, we have them," said Manuel. "You and I will have to devise something better when the need arises. Like now."

"Oh, here we go. Look at that wagon. It's dragging a whole cactus behind it in the axle. "Sergeant! Pull out and take care of that. *Ahora!* Now! And then get that wagon back in formation. *Pronto!*" commanded el capitán.

"This little hike may take longer than we thought, Capitán," laughed Manuel, riding away to see to his own squads. It was a good thing he did, too. His own men, not as disciplined as the military, were already laughing at the military's cactus fiasco and irritating the cavalrymen.

"We can't be fighting among ourselves, men," said Manuel. "So, knock off the chitchat."

Manuel rode up to his father at the head of the column.

"What was that commotion back there?" asked the don.

"Damn wagon had a cactus caught between the wheel and axle. The wheel stopped turning and was dragged. Our men thought it was very funny. Capitán Garces did not," said Manuel.

"We need to keep the friction to a minimum between our men and el capitán's, Manuel," stated Don Miguel.

"El capitán and I are well aware of that, Father," said Manuel. "El capitán and I believe that this will be a long, long trek."

"You and el capitán have no idea," said Don Miguel, under his breath. Don Miguel Peralta was the only man in the column who knew what was ahead, having been there years ago. At this point in time, he did not wish to discuss it. *My God,* thought Don Miguel. *Seven days into this expedition, and we haven't even made it to the Rio San Pedro. We must do better.*

"Manuel! Tell Capitán Garces, we march an hour earlier starting tomorrow," ordered the don.

— —

The early start seemed to help. The men did do better. They seemed to be more willing to work with each other to get the job done. Problems occurred but did not cause much delay. Don Miguel and Manuel could begin to concentrate on what lay ahead of them. There was much to consider. The summer's monsoon had ceased, giving way to blue skies. However, the temperatures of one-hundred-degrees Fahrenheit continued. Men and animals suffered from the heat. Water was the number one necessity. They could not carry all the water needed, but planning where to get more of it was important. Yet they marched on . . . and on.

— —

After many days, the procession reached the Rio San Pedro. They could refill the water casks.

Having replenished their supply of water, they could proceed northward without worrying about the water supply. The Rio San Pedro flowed south to north and therefore provided a natural watered route northward. The same river also provided water for the Indian tribes. The Yaqui, having decided that the expedition posed no threat to them, ended their surveillance. However, the Apache were very much interested in the expedition's progress. The Chiricahua band of the Apache nation controlled the whole of the area known as northern Sonora. From now on, Don Miguel's party held the attention of the Chiricahua Apache.

There were some widely scattered, very small Mexican settlements in northern Sonora. The only Mexican settlement of any size was the presidio of Tucson. The whole population of the presidio was approximately five hundred. Two hundred of that figure were military. With the Apache roving at will, there could not have been a more isolated island of civilization. The civilians had to stick close to the presidio. The expedition's route was planned to skirt well east of the presidio of Tucson. Don Miguel would rather deal with the Apache than attract attention from the ne'er-do-wells there. Don Peralta led the adventurers north, up the Rio San Pedro, hoping to eventually bypass the presidio area.

A few miles up the rio, the problems with the wagons again made themselves known. The trees and brush alongside the river allowed reasonable passage for the mounted riders, but the wagons were constantly becoming either tangled in the brush or nearly caught between the trees. Capitán Garces informed Don Miguel that, unless a wider trail was found near the river, he would have no choice but to chance the more open country west of the Rio San Pedro.

"Capitán, your suggestion . . ." began Don Miguel.

"Do not misunderstand, Don Miguel," interrupted el capitán. "This is not a suggestion. It must be done, or we will not make any time at all."

"As I was saying, Capitán Garces," stated the don, "the entire column will travel west of the river but as close as possible for protection against attack. Before sundown we must reenter the woods along the river. I will not camp in the exposed desert unless we absolutely must. Anyone who has fought the Apache would understand that fact."

"I concur completely, Don Miguel," said el capitán. "I have fought the Apache, in Chihuahua, both Chiricahua Apache and Mescalero Apache. I will increase the number of outriders on our flanks during the day."

In that moment, the expedition changed in nature from a mounted hike through the desert to a defensive, military operation. No doubt about it. The men noticed and went immediately on the alert.

6

Eventually, the expedition, still following the Rio San Pedro, made an extended camp to perform much needed repairs on wagons and equipment. They were located in semi-open terrain east of the Santa Catalina Mountains. Across the rio was a very small settlement made up mainly of farmers tending some livestock around some dilapidated adobe buildings. The people were predominantly half-breed Mexican/Indian, mostly Apache. The villagers showed only passing interest in the Peralta caravan. The travelers had no real interest at all in the village.

Capitán Garces, however, watched the activities of the villagers with great intensity. He was looking for any action that would indicate a relationship to the Apache, who were following every move of the caravan. He and Manuel were very aware that the expedition's presence had been no surprise to the villagers. He knew the Apache had marked every foot of their progress northward. He gave explicit orders that no contact was to be made between these villagers and his cavalry. Manuel gave the same orders to the Peralta miners.

Capitán Garces, from the time they first made camp near this village, had had a feeling that something was strange here. He just could not seem to put his finger on it, but he knew that something was different. As evening settled in and campfires began to be the order of camp, the two young men spoke of what was bothering el capitán. Manuel, a younger man than el capitán, had noted it and felt he must explain it to Capitán Garces.

"Capitán, we may not have to be so concerned about our men sneaking into this village and causing trouble," stated Manuel with a slight chuckle.

"How so?" asked el capitán.

"There is no reason for them to go," said Manuel. And then, with laughter, "There are no young women. Have you not noticed? They either do not have any women, or they are hiding them from us."

"Ha! You are right, Manuel. That is what was bothering me, all right. I noticed something was not right but did not realize what it was," agreed el capitán. "I doubt they don't have any young women in the village. If they are hiding them . . . oh well, I guess I cannot blame them. We look pretty dangerous, I suppose."

It seemed quite funny to Manuel and el capitán, but Don Miguel was concerned. "These people are very agitated. Something is bothering them. I will pay them a visit to find out what is wrong. Hopefully they are just apprehensive at our presence here."

— • —

Don Miguel, along with two of his trusted men from Arizpe, paid a visit to the village early the next day. They were not gone long. When they returned, Don Miguel met with Manuel and Capitán Garces. "These villagers are in bad shape. They have been robbed by both Apache and deserters from the military at the presidio of Tucson. The Apache have taken their food stores. The deserters have stolen their young women. I have left some silver coins to help them, but we must leave as soon as possible."

"Yes," agreed Capitán Garces. "If they are as desperate as you say, our livestock will tempt them even if nothing else will. *Vamanos.*"

The expedition was packed and ready in short order, and the renewed trek northward resumed within the hour. Don Miguel ordered Manuel to lead the caravan and follow the Rio San Pedro northward. He also ordered el capitán to increase the rear guard. With Manuel leading, Don Miguel took a position next to el capitán. "Capitán, I learned something from the chief of that village. He said that the deserters from the presidio left because it is rumored the presidio's federales were being ordered back south, deeper into Sonora. Such an order has not officially been given, but the desertions have begun. The deserters are not going back south-ward into Mexico. No, they are heading for California. They have heard of the gold strike. They are hiding out here, east of the presidio, to gather supplies for their trek west to California."

"That means that we must be on guard, not only from the Apache but from these deserters. These men will now be desperate and possibly more dangerous than the Apache," said Capitán Garces. "We must be alert for attacks upon our supply wagons at night."

The day wore on and the procession had moved about five miles north of the village. They were now encamped along the Rio San Pe-dro, due east of the Santa Catalina Mountains. Capitán Garces's forward scouts sent back word that they had come upon tracks of approximately a dozen shod horses . . . clearly military horses. Capitán Garces alerted Don Miguel and Manuel of this.

"Capitán Garces, Manuel, you both are military men and under-stand these deserters," said Don Miguel. "But I know and have fought the Apache in this country. I see very little difference between the Apache and these deserters. Waiting for them to make a raid on our supplies, or worse, is not to my liking."

"What do you suggest, Father?" asked Manuel, with Capitán Garces also awaiting the answer.

"I want your scouts, Capitán, to set out at dusk to locate these desert-ers. Your scouts will report to you, and, if possible, we will attack the deserters during the night. I want them all dead," replied Don Miguel.

"They have done nothing to us as yet," began Manuel, but his father, raising his hand, interrupted.

"I had planned upon avoiding, yet probably even fighting, the Apache on this trip, but I will not be additionally harassed by brigands or army deserters. I will stop them before they attack. Are your men able to accomplish this, Capitán?"

"My orders are to protect this expedition at all costs, Don Miguel. My scouts will locate them, and I will lead the attack upon them myself," assured el capitán.

Then Don Miguel added, "Manuel, you will accompany el capitán. You will assist him and obey his every command. He is in charge. I want no prisoners."

"Yes, Father," said Manuel. "If these are the same deserters who stole women from the village, what will we do with the women?"

The firelight gave an eerie, frightening aura to the look on Don Miguel's face as he spoke.

"Manuel . . . Capitán. It is my belief that the reason the women were taken has been accomplished by these animals, and the women have probably been killed. You should not have to deal with these women," said Don Miguel Peralta. "As I said before . . . no survivors."

It was after nine o'clock that night when a scout quietly slipped into the Peralta encampment. Not wishing to alarm the entire camp, he went directly to Capitán Garces. El capitán was discussing, with Manuel, possible plans concerning the attack on the deserters when the scout arrived.

"Corporal, were you able to find them?" asked el capitán.

"Sir, they are only about a mile or so up the Rio San Pedro and then a quarter mile west up a sandy wash," replied the corporal. "They are drinking tequila and are enjoying themselves. From their talk, they are planning to steal into our camp tomorrow night to relieve us of our supplies."

"Did you see any women?" queried Manuel.

"No sign of any women. But the camp is made up of several tents. If there are women, they may be in the tents," said the corporal.

Manuel and Capitán Garces looked at each other. Neither wanted to storm that camp and find women there. There was no telling the women's condition. If the women were dead, it would be better if the deserters had already done that deed. But if they were alive? *Quién sabe?* Who knows?

"I left Private Muñoz there to keep an eye on them. He will be watching for us behind a huge boulder at the side of the rio before we move up the wash," said the corporal. "Private Muñoz asks that we not shoot him by mistake," said the corporal, laughing.

"How many men will we encounter when we attack?' asked Manuel.

"I saw eleven, Capitán," relayed the corporal. "But, sir, they will be drunk or sleeping. I saw no one fit to act even as a sentry in that camp."

"Corporal, you know your men. Make sure we have four who know their job and are not afraid to do it," ordered el capitán.

"Only four, Capitán?" questioned the corporal.

"Yes. We will be eight. If we do our job well, more than half the deserters will be dead before they know they are under attack. I do not want a large squad to give away our presence before we attack," assured el capitán. Manuel had been on this type of operation before but had never told his father or el capitán. He just smiled in agreement.

"Assemble your men here in ten minutes," ordered Capitán Garces.

Within twenty minutes, the attack squad, having been briefed on their mission, quietly left the Peralta encampment area. The moon cast a bright silver glow over the desert. The squad disappeared into the shadows along the Rio San Pedro and proceeded north on foot. Capitán Garces did not want to risk any sound by riding the mile or so on horseback. The squad moved swiftly toward their target.

On the west side of the rio, rock formations shone white in the bright moonlight. One very prominent formation, standing like a great white obelisk pointing straight upward, marked the entrance to the wash. The wash was more like a canyon with a sandy bottom than a wide-open wash. During a heavy rain, this wash would be flowing with fast moving water. That night it was dry. The attack squad hardly made a sound in the sand as they moved toward the deserters' camp.

As the squad passed the white rock, the scout, Private Muñoz, who had remained in place, made his presence known. Now they were eight. Private Muñoz, without speaking aloud, signaled that the deserters were just a short way ahead. In the moonlight, he scratched a diagram of the camp in the sand. The encampment was in the center of the wash, which had widened at that point and was surrounded with brush, mainly creosote bushes. With this information, it was decided that three men would circle around to the other side of the camp to cut off any retreat further up the wash when the attack began.

Capitán Garces, with two of the men, approached the camp up the left side of the wash. Manuel and one other made their way up the right side. As they approached, they made sure that they could cover the right and left perimeters of the camp outside the tents. The squads moved to within a few feet of the tents. Six deserters were seated around the small fire, talking amongst each other. Each attacker picked his target. When Capitán Garces fired his musket, the others followed suit. The six deserters died instantly. Five other deserters charged out of the tents in utter confusion. Four were cut down by fire from the attackers' handguns. The last made the mistake of charging directly at Capitán Garces. He met his fate at el capitán's saber.

The men, in dread, searched the tents. In one tent, they found what they did not want to find . . . two women. The women could not have been older than sixteen. Both were tied. One was dead. The other was alive, but only barely. Thankfully, she was only semi-conscious. Both had been beaten and repeatedly raped.

"Mother of God!" exclaimed el capitán, momentarily stunned. He had come across similar scenes during the recent war with the United States, but he had really hoped not to see one on that night.

"Manuel, get over here!" ordered el capitán.

"I can see it from here, Capitán. What are your orders?" acknowledged Manuel.

"It is at times like this that I would rather be a peasant farmer. Have the men bury the poor dead girl. Have the corporal come in here, and we will try to make the other girl comfortable," said Capitán Garces.

"What about my father's instructions?" asked Manuel. "You heard him say 'no survivors.'"

"Your father made a bad guess. He hoped there would be no women, so that he would not be faced with—this!" exclaimed el capitán. "But we are faced with it, and now we must act on it. I am in command and must take responsibility for my decision. Private Muñoz, you and the others make up a crude litter. Corporal, bring those bastards' horses and weapons. We will not leave them to the Apache. As soon as you are ready, we will return to our camp."

Thus, just before dawn, the attack party returned to the Peralta encampment. Don Miguel Peralta was pleased and relieved that the threat from the deserters had been removed. However, the question of the survivor—the girl—must be addressed. Don Miguel said to Manuel and el capitán, "I had prayed you would find no women in that camp. This makes our travel even more difficult. But we are not barbarians. Capitán, I honor your decision. We must see to her wounds before deciding what else to do about her."

El capitán was already in motion. "Corporal, summon that horse doctor, Sergeant Mendoza, to help the girl."

The rescued girl had not uttered a word throughout this whole ordeal of attack, rescue, travel by litter, or during the medical attempt to help her. She bore silently all the effects of having been kidnapped, beaten mercilessly, and raped. She was bruised, scratched, cut, and bleeding in a dozen places. Worse, however, was the horrible blank stare from eyes that once were those of a beautiful young girl.

Sergeant Mendoza had some men rearrange one of the wagons to serve as a travelling hospital to care for the girl. Don Miguel had said, "As much as I want to, we cannot take her back to the people in that village."

"Why not?" came the expected response from both el capitán and Manuel.

"I have seen the mark on her before," said the don. "She is not one of them. She was a captive. She is Yavapai. Her tribal home is just north of our destination. I do not know how this will work for us, good or possibly bad, but I cannot bring myself to send her back to them. Let us try to save her and see what happens."

"Are the Yavapai Apache?" asked Manuel.

"No, but they are very close, often intermarrying," answered Don Miguel. "As soon as Sergeant Mendoza is ready, we must move out."

"Don Miguel, I will keep the wagon secure from visitors of any kind. Sergeant Mendoza will ride in the wagon with the girl. Two of my cavalry will be assigned to ride one on either side of the wagon. No one will be able to bother her or frighten her," stated el capitán, as he rode off to give the order.

"Manuel, you will order our miners to stay clear of that wagon. Violators will be dealt with harshly. I see nothing but trouble ahead because of this. But, as I said, 'We are not barbarians,'" Don Miguel asserted. "Get this caravan moving north!"

Don Miguel had ordered them to move north and move they did. Within a very few moments, every man—miner or soldier—had heard of the raid and its valuable cargo—the captive girl. In the ongoing wars between Indian and Mexican, nothing was so certain to provoke anger and retaliation as the taking of a captive. Every man knew it, and every man reacted with a will. No time was wasted. The terrain became less a problem now because less care was used in traversing it. The caravan just crashed through nearly every obstacle. The Peralta expedition arrived at the Rio Gila well ahead of schedule.

They took a half day off to repair some minor damage to the wagons and then proceeded as fast as possible westward along the Rio Gila. Their attention was constantly focused on the horizon on both sides of the Rio Gila. The men knew that the Apache were waiting to see what the expedition was up to, but now, having an Indian girl captive, they were terrified at the prospect of attack. The men wanted to keep moving out of sheer terror.

After the first day, the Indian girl began to show the resilience that typified her people. The eyes lost the vacant stare. She was no longer numb to the pain. Sergeant Mendoza did his best to reduce it but realized it was a sign that she was coming back to life as it were. She had actually eaten some food, but she said nothing and never took her eyes off the sergeant. Sergeant Mendoza was an older man nearing his retirement. Perhaps the girl knew that, of all these men, this man was not a threat to her. The sergeant knew that, after what she had been through, it would take time. Fear is not easily reversed.

However, fear can be a catalyst for recovery. She watched everyone's every move. Rightfully so. At an age when a girl, Indian or Mexican, should be looking forward to being a woman, dreaming of a proper husband and having a family, she was taken forcibly from her family and held captive for unknown reasons. She was then kidnapped again by the very worst of human beings, beaten unmercifully, and repeatedly raped. Why should she trust these new men?

The young girl was healing nicely. The beauty, which had been obscured by bruising, bleeding, and not being allowed to cleanse herself, was beginning to be revealed. Her face was very delicate and framed by long black hair. Her hair shone black and shiny as a raven's wing. As she healed, her dark eyes began to acquire that same shine and sparkle. Thus, as the days went by, her beauty increased. She was a very beautiful girl, indeed.

Manuel had begun to notice, as did Capitán Garces. Both men seemed to believe it to be their singular duty to see to her welfare. Both men wanted to erase the terror from her now-beautiful, dark eyes. The frequency of their inquiring visits increased to a point that Don Miguel was afraid the expedition would suffer from their lack of proper attention to it. Occasionally, their visits coincided with each other. For a while, Don Miguel just watched and shook his head. But it had become so obvious that he felt he had to stop it, even though being entertained by it, before the whole expedition suffered.

First thing one morning when both men arrived at her wagon, Don Miguel was already there to meet them. "Caballeros," began Don Miguel, "I have taken stock of the young lady's condition and have decided that she does not require the undivided attention you both have showered upon her. Your dedication to her welfare has not gone unnoticed and should be rewarded. Therefore, your reward is that I will not condemn you both in public for dereliction of duty. You will limit your visits to one per day. Please do not visit her together. I need someone I can count on to move this expedition forward. Do you both understand?"

Both men indicated agreement. But both men knew it was not over. What they did not know was that Don Miguel knew it also.

With little or no delay, the Peralta expedition moved out, westward along the Rio Gila. The desert sun, the sparse vegetation, and the ever-present dust allowed for no hiding of their movement. The Apache watched from the cover of the hillsides. They watched and waited. The Apache wanted to know the why and where of this caravan. Being unsure of the final destination was a big factor in their hesitancy to attack. Periodically, runners were sent to the Apache leaders to report the expedition's progress. So far, the Apache were unwilling to commit to attack. The expedition continued its westward movement along the Rio Gila unmolested.

Using the valley of the Rio Gila to move west of the massive mountain range east of their route, the Peralta caravan made good time. Late in the day, Don Miguel called Manuel and Capitán Garces into his tent. Both men had been wondering just how far westward they were to proceed. Don Miguel provided them the answer without having to be asked. "Caballeros, the time has come for us to move northward. Now, as never before, we must be ready to repel attack. The Apache will now realize that we are not just traveling westward toward California. They will now believe that we are going into the area of the old mines. The mines lie in an area that is both Apache and Yavapai territory. No one can be sure how or when the Apache or the Yavapai will react to this. But one thing is certain: they will react," assured Don Peralta.

"What manner of land can we expect now along the way?" asked el capitán.

"Much as you see here," replied the don. "Open desert with scattered hills. The mountains to the east will be constantly on our right flank. Be aware: the ravines running from the mountain heights down into the desert will keep us from using the shelter of the mountains for any kind of protection whatsoever. As we move farther north, along the west side of the mountains to our right, we will come to a rugged mountain the old Spanish called Sierra de La Espuma. Some are calling it 'Superstition' now. It carries with it a bad reputation for death. Even the Pima Indians of the valley floor hate and avoid it."

"Then we must travel as fast as possible in the open desert," said Manuel. "Can we count upon water along the way?"

"No. The Rio Salado is within range, but in the event of delay, we might not make it. Therefore, we must pack as much water in the casks as we can and conserve all we can as we go," said Don Miguel. "Remember, the horses and mules are most important to our mission. We must care for them first. Tomorrow, take whatever time you need to prepare. But the next morning before dawn, we move out . . . and we move out fast."

"I will make certain that we have enough outriders along the entire length of our procession. We must not allow for any surprise attack from our flanks," offered el capitán.

"Now, eat and then get a good night's sleep. You will need it," said the Don. "And, in that regard, leave the girl alone."

"Yes, sir," assured both caballeros, each looking furtively at the other, and left for the campfire and supper.

"Leave the girl alone," was Don Miguel Peralta's last order. And he meant it. But the don understood how they felt. Neither had been even anywhere near a young woman for some time. They were doing an excellent job of shepherding this armed caravan through hostile territory. They were dealing with a large force of very rough and ornery men, all day, every day.

But a young and very beautiful girl had been thrust upon them. She was also very vulnerable and hurting in body and spirit.

Both men felt their hearts go out to her. At first, they were drawn to her out of concern for her welfare. As she began to improve, her beauty began to occupy each man's thoughts. With no particular plan involved, each man set about to alleviate her fears. Friendship rapidly grew into infatuation for both.

She had spoken to no one since her rescue from the deserters, not even the sergeant. She merely indicated a *yes* or *no* by nodding her head or by a movement of her hand. The sergeant talked to her, not only because he found it pleasant to do so, but he somehow realized that it would eventually draw her out. He felt that constant conversation was most important to her eventually being able to live fully again. Sergeant Mendoza was a father himself. His concern for her was as a father for a hurt child.

The girl was not totally immune to the attention she was receiving. She realized that these were not the men who had so tormented her. The ambush at the wash was not clear in her mind. She had noticed that she was not being treated as a captive, but she also was aware that she could not leave on her own. Therefore, the definition of captive was tempered by the definition of convalescing patient.

The visits by the two young men for a while seemingly went unnoticed by her. But, as her consciousness became more acute, she began to recognize each one. However, her response to them and their visits was negligible at best. Still, time does manage to work its own small miracles. The girl, at first, hardly batted an eye in either's direction, trying to completely ignore their presence. However, she could not help but feel their concern for her welfare. She avoided their gaze but, after a few days, would raise her eyes and watch them as they left to perform their duties.

Her experience regarding any kind of courtship was, as it should have been, Indian. After all, she was Yavapai by birth and held in captivity by villagers of Mexican/Apache mixed race. Yet, as a young woman, she could not fail to recognize the interest shown in her by these two Mexican caballeros. This was very different. Yet she recognized it for what it was. Both these young men admired her. Whether or not she felt any reciprocal admiration, she began to understand that she might be able to use their admiration to her advantage someday.

The young Yavapai girl became aware that the expedition had changed direction. Now it was again moving north. She began to see familiar landmarks. The girl saw Sierra de La Espuma (Superstition Mountain) northeast of her as they trekked northward. She realized each footstep was bringing her nearer to her Yavapai people. She would do nothing now to alienate these strangers. The girl was not going to spoil her transportation home. She would put up with whatever they had in mind, at least until she was close enough to escape to the Yavapai.

Superstition Mountain

But the Peralta expedition was not there yet. They were trying to cover as much open ground as possible before any kind of attack by the Apache.

Here, the wide, heavy military wagons began to cause more trouble. The ravines and arroyos that ran downhill into the desert from the mountains began to eat the wagons as foretold. If it were possible to lay planks across the narrower ravines and cross that way, it was done. In most cases, they had to swing wide left to find a better way around them. The wagons now had to be repaired as never before. Broken wheels and axles, bent axle pins, and reloaded cargo were costing the party much downtime.

Injuries to the mules drawing the wagons had to be addressed. Some injuries were not serious; others necessitated the animal be mercifully shot. Don Miguel, Manuel, and Capitán Garces all agreed that the individual in Mexico City who ordered the use of these wagons should be unmercifully shot.

The Peralta party moved northward. In spite of everything, including the total loss of two of their eight wagons, they continued north. Mules, horses, and men were tired. The only thing that made this part of the trek more tolerable was that the intense heat had broken. The cooler temperatures of autumn had taken over.

8

In spite of the cooler weather, the Peralta expedition still needed to replenish water, rest, and regroup, thanks to the condition of the damn wagons.

They had crossed the desert, southwest of the Superstitions, without having been attacked by the Apache. No one—Neither Don Miguel Peralta, Manuel Peralta, Capitán Garces, the miners, nor the cavalry—had an answer for this.

What they could not have known was that fighting had broken out in northwestern Chihuahua and northeastern Sonora between the Mexicans and combined forces of Mescalero and Chiricahua Apache. This military confrontation would go on for nearly a year. The Apache were led by the great chief Mangas Coloradas, his son-in-law Cochise, and the great warrior chief Miguel Narbona. At the time, Cochise was a prominent subchief under Miguel Narbona. Thus, unknown to the Peraltas, great numbers of Apache warriors were involved in the conflict well southeast of the Peralta expedition. The remaining Apache, wisely, were not at liberty to attack so large and well-armed an expedition as the Peralta party.

Don Miguel Peralta, concerned for the welfare of his entire party, decided to veer off the more direct course to the Sombrero Mines. He ordered them to enter a valley that led to a box canyon on the northwest side of Superstition Mountain. Here, he remembered that water, a fall and small creek flowing in the cooler months, existed just over the east wall of the box canyon. There in that canyon, seclusion could be found.

He also believed that he could defend the canyon area by putting armed men on the surrounding perimeter walls. The expedition was able to slip into the canyon and position its defenders without incident. They were aware that the Apache had seen the move but felt the position was very defendable.

With defenses in place, the necessary wagon repairs occupied the Peralta party. Men and animals needed some repairs, too. They were all exhausted, and tempers had been flaring. Fights started at the drop of a hat, no matter who dropped the hat. Manuel, Capitán Garces, and his junior officers were hard put to keep order. It was like putting out little fires. Now the men could rest, and tempers quieted.

The Yavapai girl had been quietly progressing in her recovery. Sergeant Mendoza felt proud of his efforts and was warmed inside by her new, healthy look. He had taken on a fatherly interest in her. She could not help but realize this and would occasionally smile or touch his hand. Yet she had not uttered a word. Sergeant Mendoza asked if she had the ability to speak but was answered with only a smile.

The second evening in the canyon, Manuel Peralta and Capitán Garces just happened to arrive at the girl's wagon within a minute of each other. Yellow flowers of autumn were blooming in the canyon, and each had arrived with a similar bouquet. After watching these two vying for her attention over these last days, having them both simultaneously arrive with the same flowers evoked a smile, then a giggle, then outright laughter. For the first time, she allowed herself out of the shell that had protected her. And she obviously enjoyed it. The young gentlemen undoubtedly did.

She accepted the flowers. Manuel Peralta, younger and less reserved than el capitán, asked her name. To the surprise of all, she said in a voice smooth and sweet as a spring breeze, "U Day Ah."

El capitán, somewhat shyly asked, "Does the name have a certain meaning?"

"U Day Ah means 'the dawn' in your tongue," came the soft reply. "I have heard and know your names also. You are Capitán Garces," she said to the now smiling capitán. "You are Manuel Peralta, son of the chieftain of this caravan," she said to Manuel.

Both men were experienced with women, yet both men became somewhat tongue-tied by the sudden conversation. U Day Ah knew it, appreciated the effect she had had on these men, and began that moment to use it. U Day Ah said, "Thank you both for the flowers and your concern. I am tired now, and I must say good night."

Both men, having just been summarily dismissed, said their good nights and left. Sergeant Mendoza tried to keep from laughing but could not restrain himself. U Day Ah smiled widely at him when he said to her, "You got 'em now. Well done, girl, well done."

It had begun. For the time being, Don Miguel's order to "leave the girl alone" was put aside by the two young men. Don Miguel Peralta had other, more pressing things to oversee than to bother with supervising the two young peacocks. With the expedition encamped for a few days to retool, Manuel and el capitán saw no reason not to spend productive time with U Day Ah.

U Day Ah had begun supervised walking about the camp. Capitán Garces ordered that she was never to be allowed to wander alone. He ordered two of his older cavalrymen to accompany her when she left the wagon. However, he and Manuel managed to be available for this duty most of the time. Both young men were enjoying such walks immensely, but they did not particularly enjoy each other's competition for U Day Ah's time.

U Day Ah had regained her strength. The youthful beauty that only a young girl in her teens can possess returned to her abundantly. Her wounds were no longer visible outwardly or inwardly. When she walked, heads turned, and work stopped until she had passed. She wore her shining black hair long and straight. Sergeant Mendoza had given her a small deerskin headband, decorated with small turquoise stones. Somewhere, the sergeant had also acquired a couple of colorful Mexican skirts and blouses for her. When these clothes, her face, her hair, and her walk combined with her slim figure, the result was a radiant beauty.

Even when Don Miguel saw her, he could not blame Manuel and el capitán for being struck by her beauty. He felt the same admiration, but he also felt the inherent danger. The danger might not be from her but could very well be because of her. Once again, he just shook his head. He saw no other course but the one he was following. Let them enjoy their youth while they can.

The canyon had provided the rest they had needed. It was time to forge ahead to the Sombrero Mines. This canyon had provided shelter for the don once before when he was much younger. His gold prospectors had tried their luck years before, digging many holes but coming up with very little. The prosperous mines were yet farther north and west. The order rang out, "*Vamanos!* We go!"

The long caravan moved west, out of the mouth of the canyon and onto the desert floor. They would have to continue west to make their way around the mountains just west of the canyon. A day's travel put them at the Rio Salado. Overnighting there seemed a good idea. Camp was made even though scouts had seen some Apache on the horizon. Don Miguel knew that tomorrow they would not only have to cross the Rio Salado, but also turn north and follow the west side of the Rio Verde. Men and animals would need to be fresh in the morning.

———

Manuel and Capitán Garces had the men up, fed, and making ready to move before first light. Don Miguel Peralta, the night before at the fire, had shown Manuel a new look on his face. Manuel knew what it was. The don was realizing that they were nearing the Sombrero Mines.

Just a few more days if all went well. He was becoming excited, and Manuel could feel it with him. His father sat down for a moment with his son at breakfast. "Now, we must be alert to everything about us, Manuel," he said. "The country changes, we have a river to contend with, probable quicksand and ambush. This country is starkly beautiful, but it can kill you. Tomorrow, we begin our march up the Rio Verde. It is the country of the Yavapai. In the past, the Yavapai first avoided us, then attacked us. I do not know how they will react to us now. It is better to not provoke them. Yet we have one of their own with us. We must comport ourselves wisely."

Manuel clearly understood what his father was saying to him. He was subtly being told not to pressure the girl or antagonize her in any way. Her feelings for them now could help them or get them all killed. The don was very worried.

Manuel said, "Father, I understand and assure you that I will not betray your trust."

Don Miguel embraced him and said, "I trust you, and I am proud you are here with me."

"The men are ready," spoke el capitán as he approached them. Manuel immediately took up his position with the column of miners. Don Miguel took just a moment to discuss the matter of advancing into Yavapai country and the problem of U Day Ah. El capitán saw the wisdom and agreed with Don Miguel. "In that case, Capitán, *vamanos.*"

Later that day, because of the water level in the Rio Salado, it was decided that they would cross downstream at a point after the Rio Salado was joined by the Rio Verde. Even though the combination of the two rivers put more water into the riverbed, the riverbed was wider and shallower. Once again, the problem in crossing was those heavy wagons. Horses, mules, and men crossed rather easily. Three of the remaining six wagons clumsily made it across. The second successful wagon carried U Day Ah. Sergeant Mendoza drove it with Capitán Garces riding on one side and Manuel Peralta on the other.

The fourth wagon caught a wheel on a submerged rock and was turned sideways. The fifth wagon struck the fourth as it was turned against the current. Both wagons began to break up. The mounted men were able to rescue most of the cargo and cut the mules loose. The wagons, and pieces of wagons, floated downstream minus the wheels, which were now permanently part of the streambed.

The sixth wagon made it without incident. The chuck wagon, thankfully, made it across easily.

"Capitán Garces. Do you know where I might find the officer who mandated these oversized land barges?" queried Don Peralta.

"Yes, sir, I do," replied el capitán.

"Then never tell me. For if I know, I will surely kill him when we return," swore the don, savagely turning his horse and riding to the front of the column.

With the salvaged cargo spread over the remaining wagons and mules, the expedition pressed on up the Rio Verde. The way was not smooth.

Rough terrain forced the remaining caravan to travel, at times, with one wagon wheel in the water and the other on the bank. The delay at the river crossing forced the caravan to camp about halfway between the Rio Salado and the mouth of Camp Creek. At this point, the river spread out a bit more, and green foliage made the area seem friendlier. In spite of this, Don Peralta was still irritated because he had already had a camp picked out at the mouth of Camp Creek where it joined the Rio Verde.

Don Peralta was not the only man angry beyond speech that day. Capitán Garces was very well aware that the entire proceeding at the river crossing was not only seen as an embarrassment by his cavalry, but as a weakness by Apache scouts who were always watching. El capitán was certain that they enjoyed the spectacle. "Perhaps," he thought, "if I were not being so mindful of the girl . . ." He could not dismiss the thought that he had been negligent at least to some degree. Rightly or wrongly, he felt he had to assume some of the blame.

The next day the Peralta expedition paused to camp at the mouth of Camp Creek where it entered the Rio Verde. Don Miguel had hoped to have camped there the past night, but not stopping there now would have been a huge mistake. However, the don, knowing what actually lay ahead, was simply not ready to attack Camp Creek canyon without resting his men and animals. He also wished to spend some time in discussion with his son and with el capitán regarding the march up the Camp Creek canyon.

The site of the encampment at the mouth of Camp Creek was the ideal place to regroup. Had it not been for the delay at the Rio Salado, the party would have arrived the evening before. Don Peralta simply had to accept what happened and move forward with his plan of action. This he did. After supper, he summoned Manuel, Capitán Garces, Sergeant Mendoza, and all squad leaders, military, and miners to the central fire.

"Caballeros and compadres," began the don. "We are nearing our destination. Barring extensive problems, we should make camp in time for an early supper tomorrow night. I humbly express my gratitude to you for your valiant efforts, efforts expended simply on my word that it would be worth your while. Tomorrow, if not attacked, will still be a very hard day. Let me describe Camp Creek. I do not like to call it a creek. To me it is a glorified wash. If the winter is wet, it flows most of the year; if not, it is dry most of the year. In places, it is a narrow canyon between rock walls, as you see here. Upstream, it becomes a wide-open creosote and chaparral-studded wash. Unfortunately, the surface on which we have to travel is sand—deep, soft, unforgiving sand, interspersed with rocks. This wash is difficult enough for horses and mules to walk in, but it exhausts a man without mercy. Worse, these damn wagons are going to get bogged down. They are too heavy for the sand. I do not want to spend the whole of next week in this sand with these damn wagons! I put this to you: any ideas how we can get these clumsy log wagons through all this?"

Camp Creek

For a few moments, the silence was deafening. Then, Lieutenant Diego DaVia rose, poured himself a cup of coffee, and quietly said, "Two mules, single file, on each side of the wagon, with ropes tied to the wagon. That makes an eight-mule wagon. It should get the job done."

Again, a long silence prevailed. Then a loud, roaring laugh was heard. Don Miguel Peralta, for the first time in weeks, laughed out loud. Uproariously laughed. The walls of the canyon echoed to his laugh. Soon everyone was laughing. The don, after gasping, caught his breath and shouted, "Why did I not think of that? It is too simple. It is so simple that, of course, it will work. Ha! Lieutenant DaVia, well done! Capitán Garces, I officially request that Lieutenant DaVia be promoted. Get him another bar on his collar," directed a celebrating Don Miguel Peralta.

The end of the journey to the Sombrero Mines was in sight.

That night, a relaxed Don Miguel Peralta slept the sleep of a man whose dream is about to be realized. That night, he actually slept and slept well.

That night, U Day Ah did not.

9

U Day Ah was wide awake. She lay in the wagon that had been her bed since being rescued from her deserter captors weeks ago, but it seemed like months ago. She knew exactly where she was. All this land was very familiar to her. She had spent much of her childhood here. This encampment site was known to her people as Needle Rocks. This was very near home. She should have been very happy to see these familiar landmarks. Yet she was not. This land held many memories for her, some good, but also some memories that she had hoped to forget long ago.

Now, the wanderings of these men began to make some sense to her. Until now she had not put together the reason for, or the destination of, their journey. Now it was clear. They were heading for the old mines. She did not remember when these mines had been worked. She did remember the stories told her by her people, the Yavapai. Her people had, at first, been friendly and welcoming to the strange men who wandered the hills looking for the yellow stones. They had wondered why these men wanted these stones so much that they were willing to work so hard to get them from the Earth Mother. Many Yavapai, when told that the men wanted only to make other places beautiful with the stones, agreed to help them pull the stones from the washes and holes in the hillsides.

The Yavapai men were given the firewater as a gift for their help. Soon, the Yavapai men of her village were as crazy men because of the firewater. The Yavapai who did not work digging the yellow stones ran away to the north. Those who were not able to run became as slaves to work the mines. They were whipped and beaten and guarded at all times by both the Spanish and, later, the Mexicans.

The girl, U Day Ah, remembered now all the horrible stories told by her people about the men with the whips. She remembered the stories of how the Yavapai, with their Apache cousins, began fighting back. Groups of Yavapai began to attack the small parties of miners as they left their main camp to work the numerous holes in the hillsides. The local Yavapai band was small in number. The main body of Yavapai was many miles to the north. Yet many, when they heard the cries of their people, came forth to help against the miners.

It was then that the miners packed their gold and equipment and headed south, out of the land of the Yavapai. The Yavapai celebrated what they thought was the end of the miners in their country, but now the miners were back, and U Day Ah was with them!

U Day Ah must not be found with these miners! She knew that the Yavapai would think that she had become one of them, or worse, that she had become the sexual plaything of these men. She must escape.

Her memory of this place was many years old but became clearer as the minutes passed. Shortly after she had been captured by a wandering party of Tonto Apache, they had camped in this very spot, Needle Rocks. She was but a girl of about twelve years old. She was captured while gathering berries. After leaving their camp at Needle Rocks, the Apache sold her to some Pima Indian villagers who lived south in the valley of the Rio Salado. Many months later, she was sold to the villagers where she had been kidnapped by the deserters from the presidio of Tucson.

She must escape! Now!

As the celebration began to wind down, and men began to seek sleep, she slowly moved through the shadows to the outer perimeter of the camp. Here the Rio Verde flowed from north to south. On the north side of the camp, past the rock formations that gave the site its name, she slipped quietly into the water. The water was not more than a couple feet deep, and the current was not too swift. She crossed to the east shore in order to render her trail impossible to follow on the camp side of the river. Once across, she stayed in the water while moving upstream. She did not have any idea how far her people were, but she knew they were to the north. It was not easy, but northward she went. She was a mile up-river when she thought it was safe to leave the water and proceed on land.

U Day Ah kept to the east side of the river, fearful that she could be followed. Had she stayed on the west side, any pursuers might more eas-ily find her tracks. She followed the Rio Verde until well past midnight. Finding a clear area on a sand bar, she lay down to rest. Exhausted, but exhilarated by her freedom, she actually slept. She slept until just before dawn. Using a mesquite branch, she swept away her markings in the sand. She was very hungry but pressed on following the Rio Verde. She knew that by keeping to the edge of the Rio Verde as the sun arose, she would be unseen in the long shadows of dawn. She made good time. U Day Ah was not hampered by wagons and tough going as the Peralta miners would be that morning. As she stealthily made her way upriver, she kept a sharp eye out for both pursuers and, hopefully, Yavapai. The entire first day of her freedom she saw neither.

10

The celebration, after Lieutenant DaVia's brilliant idea to use extra mules to pull the wagons up the deep sandy wash, had begun to wind down. Most of the men, miners and military, were looking for a good place to bed down for the night. Sentries had been relieved for the night shift. The fires were burning down to embers.

Manuel Peralta was feeling about as relieved as he had ever felt during this long trek. Indian scouts had not been seen for two days now. He felt that this was a good sign. Manuel did not like any part of being watched day and night by Chiricahua Apache. Besides, he was just plain tired. But, before retiring to his bedroll, he felt he should check on U Day Ah. He had not seen her during all the happy bantering around the campfires. Aside from making sure she was all right, Manuel just wanted to say good night to the lovely young woman.

Manuel had no sooner arrived at her wagon when Capitán Garces stepped up from the other direction. They came upon each other so abruptly that each was startled. "What the . . . ?" exclaimed el capitán as Manuel exclaimed, "Oh, no, not you tonight!"

"U Day Ah—are you awake?" asked Manuel.

Both men became concerned when no reply came from the wagon.

"Sergeant Mendoza, are you in there?" asked el capitán.

"I am here, behind the wagon, sir," came the reply.

"Where is U Day Ah?" both young men asked.

"I thought she was in the wagon just a few minutes ago," said the sergeant.

"Sergeant, you and two others circle the perimeter of the camp looking for her. Manuel and I will go the other way. Whoever finds her, or her tracks, let the others know, but do not do it by firing your gun," ordered Capitán Garces. "I do not want the whole camp up and shooting."

After about fifteen minutes, both parties met once again at the wagon. "There are no signs of violence. No signs of anything," reported the sergeant. "There are so many tracks in the sand, and it is so dark. I do not know."

"If she meant to escape by way of the river, she probably made a good job of it," said Manuel. "Capitán, do you agree that our chances of finding her trail tonight are nonexistent?" asked Manuel Peralta.

"There is not even a prayer of locating her trail tonight," agreed el capitán.

"Then I will inform Don Miguel first thing in the morning. There is no sense disturbing him now," said Manuel.

———

The next morning, Don Miguel Peralta, expecting to begin the last couple days' march to el Sombrero Mines, was jolted into anger upon hearing Manuel's news. "She what!" he shouted. "When?"

"Sometime just before the celebrating ended," replied Manuel.

"Where was Sergeant Mendoza? Was he not guarding her?" loudly asked Don Miguel.

"Sergeant Mendoza was assigned to care for her during her injury, not guard her from leaving," said Manuel. "He has done that faithfully."

"I thought you and el capitán would be all over her competing for whatever you had in mind for her. Where the hell were you both?" yelled Don Miguel, extremely agitated.

"We were both with you, Father, at the fire, celebrating," answered Manuel.

"She is Yavapai! We are in Yavapai country! Someone had better find her tracks and bring her back, or we could have very little to celebrate from now on!" exclaimed the don.

Private Muñoz, along with el capitán, stepped slowly near Don Peralta and Manuel as they were speaking. El capitán said, "Pardon this interruption, Don Miguel. Private Muñoz has been trying to find U Day Ah's trail since dawn. Tell him what you found, Private."

"Just north of our camp, maybe one hundred steps, I found a partial footprint. It was small and was right at the water's edge. I could find no other sign," said Private Munoz.

"Which direction would she be heading?" asked Don Miguel.

"I could find no indication. I know you do not want just a guess, Don Peralta," said the private. "But it seems to make sense to me that she would be heading upstream. I could find no tracks leading out of the river on this side."

Don Peralta, having regained his composure, said, "Thank you, Private Muñoz. You have done well. I agree with your guess. For her to go downstream, from whence we have just come, would make no sense. U Day Ah is trying to find her people."

El capitán dismissed Private Muñoz and, after he had gone, addressed Don Peralta. "I must apologize, Don Miguel, for my laxness in not assigning a sentry to watch her movements. It very well may prove to have been a bad mistake on my part, and I alone accept the blame."

"Capitán Garces, I have already expressed my anger at my son. I do not feel compelled to repeat it again to you," calmly stated the don.

"If you wish, I will send out patrols to search for U Day Ah on the other side of the rio," said el capitán.

"No, Capitán. That would simply waste more time. That search would not have a chance of finding her anyway. She has a six, maybe eight-hour head start. Even if she stayed at the rio's edge, we would waste two days at least finding her," said Don Peralta. "Capitán, I will need you to provide security, front, rear, and on both flanks as we proceed up this canyon. I want outriders atop the ridges on both sides of the canyon until it flattens out into the great wash ahead," ordered the don.

"Yes, Don Miguel," agreed el capitán. "Immediately."

"Manuel, organize your miners. Go with Lieutenant DaVia's idea to use the ropes to add mules to each wagon, get this train moving," ordered Don Miguel.

"Neither you, nor I, have had any breakfast, Father," stated Manuel.

"Breakfast? The wagon eating sand in this canyon bottom is going to make a morning's ride into a three-day nightmare. We will eat tonight in camp, hopefully at least a third of the way to our destination," stated the irritated Don Miguel. *"Vamanos! Pronto!"*

Manuel Peralta, as per his father's orders, without breakfast, began the process of attaching ropes to the sides of the wagons. Extra horse collars, from the wagons lost at the Rio Salado crossing, were now implemented to attach the ropes to the extra mules. This was no small task. Ropes had to be measured to uniform lengths for each mule pulling alongside the wagon. Otherwise, some sideways pulling could tip the wagon. The one wagon that none of the men wished to see tipped over was the chuck wagon. It took the better part of an hour to accomplish this task.

Miners, horses, mules, wagons, and cavalry started up the canyon, northwesterly from Needle Rocks. The wheels of the wagons, carrying as much cargo as the men had been able to salvage from the Rio Salado crossing debacle, sank deeply into the sand. But Lieutenant DaVia's rope idea was paying off. The wagons moved slowly, but without the problems that could have occurred due to the deep, soft sand of the canyon floor.

Hearts had been high that last night. The celebrating was a much-needed break from the toil that had been theirs for the past month. They had been told that their destination, the Sombrero Mines, was within a couple days' ride. The steep canyon walls of Camp Creek would surely offer them the opportunity to complete their journey without being watched by whatever Indian tribe was out there.

However, the situation had changed with the escape of the Yavapai girl, U Day Ah. Until then, the men—miners and cavalry—had thought of her just as an attractive young Indian woman, pretty to look at while walking around the camp at the evening meals. U Day Ah was indeed pretty to look at, and most of the men would have been happy to have more than just a look at her, even for just a while. But none of the men had been stupid enough to try anything except a shy greeting as she walked by them. She was, after all, a captive of the Peralta expedition. It was obvious that both Manuel Peralta and Capitán Garces each considered her his own. None of the men, miner or military, wished that kind of confrontation. She was simply not for them.

Now, however, U Day Ah had become to them just an escaped Yavapai Indian, possibly bent on causing the expedition great harm. Would she be the cause of a Yavapai attack? No one knew, but all feared so. The entire trip had been filled with the vision of Yaqui, then Apache watching their every move. They had not attacked. Why? Had U Day Ah come to trust the men of the Peralta expedition? Would she be a messenger of friendship? Most of the men did not think that. The men all feared that her hatred of those who had so greatly abused her would cause her to hate all non-Yavapai. Would that hatred be unleashed upon them by U Day Ah's own Yavapai?

All the men could do for the moment was to work feverishly to get the Peralta expedition to the Sombrero Mines as quickly as possible, if for no other reason than their own safety. There, they believed, they could build positions from which to defend themselves. Whips cracked, mules brayed, and horses snorted as they made their way through the deep sand. The mules and horses did not like that deep sand any more than the men. It made for extremely difficult walking, much less pulling.

The canyon was by no means straight. It was narrow and rocky for the first few miles with sudden switchbacks. The canyon was constantly turning, first left, then right, just to continue in a generally northwesterly direction. These switchbacks, not only difficult to maneuver, were natural, very effective spots for ambush. But the ambush never came. Capitán Garces had placed scouts to patrol the ridgetop along both sides of the canyon. That effectively prevented any surprise attack from the ridgetops, as well as any possible ambush attacks at those switchbacks. El capitán gained even more respect for Don Miguel's grasp of military strategy. El capitán would have done that anyway, but it was significant to him that Don Miguel had insisted on it first. Evidently, Don Miguel Peralta had had experience in his past involving such matters, about which he did not speak.

The weather was cool, and the sun was shining. It would have been noted by the men of the caravan as a very pleasant day had they not been working so hard. The fear of the unknown pushed them on without respite. Even though plodding through the sand was like swimming against a very strong current, the caravan moved on. The expedition exited the canyon into a wide open wash, studded with creosote bushes and mesquite. The canyon walls were now wide apart so that the caravan could move in a fairly straight manner. Security still had to be tightly maintained. Any attacking party could be well-concealed by the bushes in the wash.

In spite of the difficulty in traversing the deep sand of the wash, the extra mules drawing the wagons resulted in the caravan making better time than the don had expected. Two days later, sunset found them in a wide-open area of the wash adjacent to a mountain of gray-blue color. The Yavapai called it Blue Mountain.

Blue Mountain

Camp was hastily made, but security was not forgotten. The guard was doubled on the camp perimeter. One patrol route was close to the camp and the other about two hundred feet farther out. The patrols walked their routes in opposite directions. If an attack occurred, it would not come as a surprise.

Don Miguel Peralta joined Manuel Peralta and Capitán Garces at supper.

"Tomorrow, caballeros, we will make a final camp at the entrance to the hills protecting the Sombrero Mines. We are within sight of the hills that protect them. We will be there before noon tomorrow. We will have an excellent start at retrieving gold from these mines. There is much gold yet to be mined, and we will mine as much of it as we can carry," asserted the don.

The two caballeros smiled and patted each other on the back.

"The only factor that has worried me since planning this expedition has been the Indian threat," continued Don Miguel. "I was fully prepared to accept the probability that we would have to fight them for this gold. The Yavapai girl's presence here was unforeseen and has become a problem. I had hoped that she would acclimate to our group, perhaps perform cooking or cleaning chores to help become one of us. Her wounds healed, and it was noted that she admittedly is a beautiful young woman. You two must have noticed that fact. You treated her as an object of affection, at least sexually. You evidently created a feeling, on her part, that she was special to you. You, also, felt that she was special.

"Well, she was so special that you allowed her the run of the camp, so that escape presented her no particular problem," said Don Miguel, very upset.

"I tried to show her that we were not the animals that brutalized her," asserted Manuel. "Both el capitán and I tried to show her nothing but kindness and concern."

"I can speak for myself, Manuel," interrupted el capitán. "It is true, Don Miguel. I felt affection for her. Yes, she is much younger than I, but I felt something for her beyond lust. I was hoping . . . well you know what I was hoping. It is my fault that she is no longer in camp."

"I, too, Father, felt as did el capitán. You must admit her beauty was beyond compare," said Manuel.

"Yes," said Don Miguel. "But from the start, you knew she was Yavapai. You knew that she was of the tribe that will deeply resent our return to our mines. Someday, starting now, you'd better stop thinking with your crotch. You—we all—may be killed because you two failed to use your head. Pray that none of us ever sees her again. For if we do, it is not likely that she will be alone. Start using your head. That is an order! *Comprende?*"

"Yes, sir!" was the answer of both men.

—•—

The don was correct. The next morning, the caravan reached the site of what was to be their main encampment. It was on a low hill out of the wash on the southwest side. Here the wash ran with a supply of water flowing from the mountain ridges above them. On the hillside above the site stood a great stone, the size of three wagons standing on end straight up. This stone was formed in the shape of a man's head. The don remembered from the old days that the Yavapai and the Apache both believed this stone to have some religious significance. This fact he did not pass on to any of the men, not even Manuel or el capitán.

The rock in the shape of a man's head

Don Miguel Peralta also did not inform anyone that on top of the hill above the Rock in the Shape of a Man's Head were numerous circles of rocks. These rocks had, in ancient times, been the homes of possibly the ancestors of the Yavapai. The Yavapai did not know, nor did the Apache, but the fact that they were the Ancient Ones made the area sacred to both tribes. One could surely expect trouble.

Don Miguel Peralta, without giving any reason, demanded that orders be given that no one venture on top of that hill. No one. In order to ensure this, Don Miguel instructed Capitán Garces to make sure that a double guard was placed around the entire hill.

11

U Day Ah had not rested since crossing the Rio Verde and moving northward. The Rio Verde made a great bend, first east, then north, then westward again, as it flowed ever from the north. The river continued its twisting, winding path. U Day Ah followed its meandering path for three days. She followed the winding Rio Verde, never leaving its bank. She knew that eventually it must lead to her people.

The Rio Verde

But she was so very hungry. She was used to meager meals, but to not have any meals . . . Some plants helped fend off her hunger, but only for a while. Her hunting skills were poor, so she had to make do with whatever she could find. It was hard on her, but U Day Ah was free! Maybe only free to die here beside this desert river, but free, nonetheless.

From a hilltop, she could see the river make its great bend back again to the north. It was so tempting for her to leave the river and go cross-country. It would have saved her some miles of following the river. She was so tired and weak from not eating, but she knew she could not attempt it. The desert is unmerciful and unforgiving, so she doggedly and wisely kept to the riverbank and walked on and on and on.

U Day Ah tried to keep going at night, but after the third night she exhaustedly fell asleep on a great flat rock that jutted out into the river. It was not the time of year for snakes, so her unconscious sleep was unmolested. She slept the entire night. Her dreams were not peaceful, as memory kept interrupting. She became aware of the bright light of the sun. She should have been awake and moving by now. Yet as she had been disturbed by the morning light, she was startled by a shadow falling upon her face. Her eyes snapped open to behold the face of a warrior, a Yavapai warrior.

She made no sound as he carried her to his horse and placed her upon it. Before mounting it himself, he gave her some deer jerky to eat. Remembering her training as a Yavapai woman, she graciously took it and began eating it slowly, even though she was hungry enough to eat the horse upon which she was sitting. The warrior smiled, mounted, and quietly urged his horse northward.

It was near midday when the warrior lowered the sleeping girl into the arms of the Yavapai women who reached up to receive her. She was taken, still sleeping, into the wikiup of the ranking woman of the camp.

The Yavapai camp was small, consisting of approximately twenty people. Five wikiups provided shelter for them all. The camp was located on the east bank of the Rio Verde at the point where the river flowed out of the mountain range that stretched far to the north. Here the band had been camped for about a week, hunting and fishing the gently flowing Rio Verde. There were mostly women and children at this camp; five or six warriors and their families made up the entire group.

The young warrior who found and returned U Day Ah was not a part of this camp family. He was from a Yavapai band under the warrior chief Nanni Chaddi. The warrior was named O hi Cama (Striking the Enemy). He was young but was becoming as adept and fearless as Nanni Chaddi. He would soon become a subchief of the Yavapai. As for now, he was content to rest himself with this band while the girl slept. She slept all that afternoon and all that night.

U Day Ah awoke the next morning in the wikiup where she had been taken. She remembered nothing after being put on the warrior O hi Cama's horse. She inadvertently let out a shriek upon seeing unfamiliar surroundings. Hearing her, the women of the camp rushed to her. It took but a moment to calm her. Hearing her native tongue spoken by the women reassured her that she was at long last safe with her own people.

The women took her outside the wikiup so that she could see where she was and lose her fear. She stood, looked at the wikiups of this small band of her people, and felt at home again. She smiled and accepted the bowl of food offered to her. Her eyes moved over the camp, the river, the surrounding hillsides, the women of the camp, and the children who were gazing in some awe at her. She smiled at them and laughed at their shy scurrying out of her gaze. The few men in the camp waited as she looked at them and then politely went back to their fishing.

U Day Ah's gaze stopped abruptly when she saw the warrior O hi Cama. She saw him standing about ten paces from her. She looked at him closely. He was tall and lean but muscular. He held his head high and did not turn his eyes from her as had the other men. He was a very impressive warrior. She liked what she saw, and she noticed that he was looking appreciatively at her also.

It was then she realized that her appearance was not up to her potential. She needed considerable tender loving care to bring back her natural beauty. Before O hi Cama could turn away, U Day Ah dashed back into the wikiup with tears in her eyes. O hi Cama immediately sensed her embarrassment. He turned, mounted his horse, and left the village at a slow gait. He did not turn his gaze backward, not wishing to cause her any more concern. She had been through enough. He had no idea what, but he knew she was hurting inside and out. He thought he might just have a look downriver.

O hi Cama slowly guided his pinto downstream along the bank of the slow-moving Rio Verde. He had no trouble finding the place where he had found the girl. Her efforts to leave no trail might have been good enough to avoid discovery by the miners, but not by O hi Cama. He very easily followed her trail back to where she had exited the water just north of Needle Rocks. Not a trace of her trail now existed on the east bank of the river, so he slowly rode across toward Needle Rocks.

What he saw shocked the young Yavapai warrior. Tracks of men, animals, and wagons were everywhere. Shod horses and mules, men's boot tracks, and wagon tracks. There were so many that he could not even guess their number. O hi Cama had no direct experience with Mexicans, but he knew these could be the evidence of no other men. A huge party of Mexicans had camped here. But why?

The girl must have been with them and had either escaped or been driven off by these men. It was getting late, but he had to follow these tracks. After all, a party of this size was not just passing through. He must find out who these men were and where they were headed and why. And why had the girl been with them?

O hi Cama's warrior heart was beating wildly as he began following the immense trail up Camp Creek canyon. He was not afraid of these men, but he was greatly awed by the obvious size of their expedition. The tracks were a few days old. The Yavapai was not afraid that he would catch up with them soon. He merely wanted to follow them far enough to ascertain something of their destination. He followed the trail until it left the protection of the canyon walls and emptied out onto the wide dry wash.

He reined his pinto to an abrupt halt. A memory of old tales of the Mexicans who tore the yellow stones from the Earth Mother rushed into his mind. Without hesitation, he urged his pinto up and over the ridge on the northeast side of the canyon. Once on top of the ridge, he rode at a quick lope, cross-country, to the Yavapai camp and the girl.

During the time of O hi Cama's absence, the local women had wasted no time. U Day Ah had been scrubbed, preened, and primed to be able to greet any young man proudly. Her hair had been washed and brushed to its gloriously black sheen. Her skin showed the ripe glow of her youth.

She had been presented with a lightweight doeskin dress of one of the other women of the camp. The turquoise necklace and earrings were not needed to bring forth her natural beauty. She was radiant. The women had returned to her the pride of Yavapai womanhood.

This was the vision of U Day Ah seen by O hi Cama as he slowly rode into the camp. He first saw her in the firelight as he dismounted his pinto. For a long moment his eyes were seeing nothing else. Her eyes, her face, with the hint of a smile, merely added to the vision of her young curves, accentuated by the soft doeskin dress. That image of her would never leave his memory.

He was tired but needed some answers to a few questions before he could ride on to find Nanni Chaddi. O hi Cama walked directly to the campfire and U Day Ah. He paused but a moment before saying, "How many Mexicans have come into our land?"

U Day Ah's answer came without hesitation: "Over two hundred, maybe even fifty more."

"Why are they here?" was his next question.

"They are here for the yellow stones. Gold," she replied.

"Why were you with them?" was O hi Cama's very predictable question.

U Day Ah began to say but hesitated and then said, "I was not with them. I was injured and a captive. They saved me and cared for me. I will tell you more after you are rested. Sleep now. We will speak more tomorrow."

U Day Ah was normally an early riser, but the next morning when she arose from sleep, O hi Cama was already gone. Evidently, he had heard enough to warn Nanni Chaddi of the incursion into their land. He had seen no reason for delay. U Day Ah was not sure why, but her heart sank. She thought it was because she was unable to completely explain her presence with the Mexicans. At first, she could not understand why it should matter to her, but it did.

O hi Cama was not sure where Nanni Chaddi would be when he left the Yavapai camp. He was hoping he would be in the higher country a short distance to the north. The upcoming winter would not be severe in the area of the Yavapai camp on the Rio Verde, but upriver preparations must be made to survive the expected cold and snow. Hopefully, Nanni

Chaddi would be somewhere in that vicinity. He was right. After night-fall, O hi Cama spotted the campfires of Nanni Chaddi's band.

He approached carefully. Although deep in Yavapai country, Nanni Chaddi was not one to let down his guard. After all, as chieftain he was the protector of his people. He did not shrink from war, but he also took no chances with the security of his band. Knowing this, O hi Cama began to make his presence known well before trying to enter the camp. Once identified, he asked to see Nanni Chaddi. O hi Cama was no stranger to these people and was brought to Nanni Chaddi immediately. He asked that they speak in the privacy of his wikiup.

O hi Cama and Nanni Chaddi would normally exchange pleasantries at this meeting, but O hi Cama came directly to the reason for his visit. "My chieftain, a large force of Mexicans has entered our land."

"How many?" asked Nanni Chaddi moving forward. "Why do they come?"

"Well over two hundred men. They have wagons. The tracks are deep in the sandy wash. They have brought with them much equipment and supplies. They come to take more of the yellow stones from Earth Mother," related O hi Cama.

"Where do they come for the stones?" slowly asked Nanni Chaddi.

"Their tracks lead up the canyon and wash from Needle Rocks. Plain-ly, they are heading for the sacred places near the Rock in the Shape of a Man's Head where the Ancient Ones lived," said O hi Cama somberly.

"I was but a very young warrior when these men were driven from our land. We offered them friendship and help. The Mexicans thought only of the yellow stones. They were cruel to our people. They respected nothing of our people. They believed we were a lesser race. Our people were made to endure digging for the yellow stones. Those who refused were whipped and worse. Our women were defiled. We had to hide them in the high country," Nanni Chaddi related with tears in his eyes.

He continued. "We fought them and lost many warriors. In the end, they ran. We showed them the lesser race of men. They ran like rabbits from our land. Even the other Mexicans to the south did not enter our land again. Now, even as we hear they also soon will leave the south, these men come." His voice rose in anger as he spoke.

"What shall we do, my chieftain?"' asked O hi Cama.

"I do not know," said the chief. "We are few now and scattered over a large part of our land. You speak of over two hundred men, well supplied. What do you suggest, O hi Cama?"

"I would first put our thoughts to a council. Then wait. Let the Mexicans struggle through the winter. Let them expend their supplies. Watch them closely. Give ourselves time to see how to again drive them from the land of the Yavapai," said O hi Cama.

"You are young, but there is wisdom in your words," replied Nanni Chaddi. "I will send riders to our outlying bands to call a council here at the full moon. Now, O hi Cama, rest yourself. I can see you are tired. You have done well."

12

Having taken O hi Cama's words to heart, Nanni Chaddi sent couriers to the various bands of the Yavapai, requesting a council at the full moon. O hi Cama had briefly told him of the girl and how she came to return to her people. He knew she had much more to tell, and he desperately wanted to hear what she could relate. It was a long day's ride, but at the end of the day he and O hi Cama entered the Yavapai camp on the Rio Verde.

The warriors of the camp were pleased and honored to have their chieftain in their camp. The women gave them food and drink. All waited around the main campfire to hear all that was new in their world. They heard plenty. When the incursion of the Peralta expedition was first stated, a great cry went up from those at the campfire. A sharp look from Nanni Chaddi silenced it. They all now respectfully sat to hear more. Nanni Chaddi and O hi Cama related only the basics of the information they already knew.

A shelter was made ready for Nanni Chaddi and O hi Cama. When all was ready and most were ready to settle down for the night, U Day Ah arrived at the small wikiup. The three sat outside. No words were spoken for a while. Then, Nanni Chaddi spoke softly to U Day Ah.

"U Day Ah, I understand that you accompanied the Mexicans into our land. I need to know all that you can tell me for me to be able to decide wisely how to protect our people. Do not fear me or any other Yavapai. You are one of us. You are Yavapai. You have suffered but have survived and returned to us. And you are welcomed to your home," assured Nanni Chaddi.

"Surviving among people who are not your own is an admirable feat. How you survived and whatever you had to do to survive is justified by your very presence here with us tonight. So be open, honest, and unashamed in relating your story to us. Because we are your people, Yavapai, we understand. Please, tell us now all that you can," directed Nanni Chaddi.

U Day Ah started to stand out of respect for her chieftain to tell her story but was told to sit and be comfortable. After all, they were all family here. She began her tale by asking if the hostilities between the Yavapai and the Tonto Apache were ended. She was assured no hostilities existed between the Yavapai and the Tonto Apache. Relieved, she related that when she was about twelve summers, she had slipped out of camp to gather berries. It was early, and dew was still on the plants. She heard a great shout: war cries, screams of pain and death. Then, all was silent. Suddenly, she felt herself swept up onto a pony and carried away. She tried to leap off the pony, but the warrior who grabbed her struck her unconscious with his war club. She awakened in the camp of about twenty warriors of the Tonto Apache.

She was taken to the main village, quite a distance from her own Yavapai country, on top of a long precipice. She was in the "Mogollon Rim" country of the Tonto Apache. U Day Ah was made to work hard and was beaten if she did not please the women in charge. She was considered too young to be given to any warrior. For this reason, she was taken south into the desert country west of Sierra de la Espuma. There she was sold to a band of Pima who raised most of their own food in that desert valley.

But she was Yavapai. U Day Ah tried repeatedly to escape. The Pima tired of her and sold her to some wandering half-caste Apache/Mexicans. Her life became even worse among them. They considered themselves neither Mexican nor Apache. They were nothing as a people. They treated her as a slave. She was blossoming into puberty by now and keeping the young (and older) men away from her became another problem. She was a pretty, young teenager. U Day Ah ashamedly admitted that occasional rape had occurred. At this revelation, she was reassured to see nothing but compassion in the eyes of Nanni Chaddi and O hi Cama. In O hi Cama's eyes she thought she saw something else also—pain.

Then, in the Santa Catalina Mountains east of the presidio of Tucson, a group of Mexican cavalry soldiers entered the village. At first, it was thought that all they wanted was water and information. Then, a fight started. Most of the villagers ran away, leaving the women and girls to fend for themselves. U Day Ah and another young teenage girl were carried off by these soldiers. If the girls could have found a way to kill themselves, they would have done so. Instead, they were subjected to three days and nights of repeated beatings and rape by many men. Mercifully, unconsciousness relieved their suffering. The other girl did not survive.

Sudden gunfire, which U Day Ah barely was able to recognize, erupted outside the tents. In seconds, all eleven soldiers were dead. Others swept her out of the tent, tried to bind her wounds, and spirited her to their camp. It was the Mexican miners, the Peralta expedition.

U Day Ah told of the care and later the attention given to her as the expedition moved ever northward. She told of the conversations she overheard about the yellow stones and how important it was to get all they could as fast as they could and then to return to their homes in southern Sonora. She told of the rest stop at the box canyon near La Sierra de la Espuma. The Mexicans felt that they were safe there in that place.

She minimized the tale of her escape along the Rio Verde at Needle Rocks with the exception of her gratitude to O hi Cama for her rescue from the effects of hunger and exhaustion. She praised him greatly for returning her to her people, the Yavapai.

She was about to ask Nanni Chaddi if he knew what had happened to her family as a result of the initial attack by the Tonto Apache, when he interrupted her. He merely said that she was the only survivor of the attack. She sadly lowered her head. He then added, "There was no war. You had been taken by a renegade band exiled from their people."

Nanni Chaddi leaned forward and, with both hands, lifted her face. "U Day Ah, bad things happen when enemies are about. You have seen and lived through the worst of it. You must feel no shame. You should be praised. You must walk forward in your life as if none of those things have happened to you. You are free of blame. You must consider yourself, as we do for you, free of any taint. You are the best example of a Yavapai woman. Welcome to your home."

Through tear-filled eyes, U Day Ah could see the face of O hi Cama. Unashamedly, as he looked upon her, she saw his own eyes filled with tears.

— ▪ —

The next morning, Nanni Chaddi and O hi Cama bade farewell to the small camp on the Rio Verde. It was their purported intention to head back up the Rio Verde northward to where O hi Cama had found the chief just two nights earlier. The two Yavapai left riding in that direction, but when out of sight of the camp, they veered sharply southwest in the direction of the Rock in the Shape of a Man's Head and of the Peralta encampment.

Their goal was to quietly see what their adversary looked like. They needed to see first-hand what they would be up against. The distance was not all that far, but the desert was very difficult and rough. Ravines and cactus-studded pathways made the going longer than anticipated. Late afternoon found them looking from a distance at the hill that had once housed the Ancient Ones. Leaving their horses, they made their way on foot. They did not want to be seen yet by the miners. They crossed the ridge, went over Camp Creek, then up the ridge on the south side of Camp Creek. This placed them looking across a second wash directly opposite the Rock in the Shape of a Man's Head.

What they saw left them speechless. The Peralta miners, two hundred strong, had put up a strong perimeter of defense around the area. It was not stockade but might as well have been. Wagons, bales, boxes: anything that could hinder an attacker from entering the camp was in place. Guards were walking their posts. Very impressive. What startled the two Yavapai warriors was that these guards were uniformed, armed professional soldiers. This was not just a gang of undisciplined miners. These two hundred miners were guarded by a strong military force of about fifty cavalry.

Nanni Chaddi and O hi Cama had seen all they wanted to see and more. They looked at each other without speaking, nodded, and slowly backed down the ridge. Once out of sight of the encampment, they mounted their horses and slowly, without raising any dust, rode back toward the camp of Nanni Chaddi's band. They must have time to gather their thoughts before discussing with others what they had seen at the Peralta camp.

To the Yavapai, who spent their lives in small bands scattered over a large expanse of countryside, the presence of such a large, concentrated force as the Peralta expedition was daunting to say the least. Plans must be made to deal with this incursion, but efforts must be made to not allow panic within the Yavapai. Both Yavapai warriors contemplated the situation quietly to themselves as they slowly rode to their camp.

———

They arrived very late the next day to the camp of Nanni Chaddi, spoke of what they had seen to no one, and fell into an exhausted yet fitful sleep. When they awoke, the villagers politely did not press them as to what they had seen. Within the week, the participants in the requested council of Yavapai bands would convene. Therefore, whatever was happening would be resolved then, or so they thought. In the meantime, Nanni Chaddi and O hi Cama went about their business as if nothing eventful was happening.

———

A few days later, the first of the subchiefs of the Yavapai began to arrive at the village. They had not been told the object of the council but dressed in their most stylish and colorful clothing, expecting some sort of festivities. Nanni Chaddi greeted them all warmly and indeed treated them to feasting and dancing. This lasted well past the arrival of the last of the subchiefs.

Early in the morning, after the last night of socializing, the flap of the council wikiup closed. At that point, the celebrating ceased. Having greeted all the subchiefs, Nanni Chaddi sat down and allowed O hi Cama to address the gathering. He spoke in a tone deliberately subdued, so as not to unduly alarm the council members, but emphasized the various points as to what the Yavapai were facing.

The people of the village could not hear exactly what was said within the council wikiup. The tone of the voices conveyed the excited speeches of the council members. The people could not help but feel the anger and fear expressed inside. The villagers became silent as the uproar inside escalated. Soon it was noted that silence had taken over inside the council wikiup.

The council members, on recommendation by O hi Cama, had decided to bide their time. Time would be the Yavapai's great secret weapon. It was Nanni Chaddi's thought that winter would bring stress and some measure of hardship to the strange intruders. It would also give the Yavapai time to gather warriors into the area from the many outlying areas of their country. After the winter, the Yavapai would begin a war of harassment against the Peraltas. All this would take time. The Yavapai would use this time to possibly make an alliance to drive the Peraltas from their midst.

The younger Yavapai had to be shouted down by the older, more responsible warriors because they wanted to attack immediately. The older warriors saw the wisdom in O hi Cama's and Nanni Chaddi's plan. Biding their time would make victory possible. Each band would act in concert with the directives of Nanni Chaddi through O hi Cama. O hi Cama had, in a very short time, achieved the status of Nanni Chaddi's *warrior in charge*.

O hi Cama's first orders were that scouting patrols of two warriors each were to patrol the area of the Peralta camp to report any activity of the miners and soldiers. Any and all information gathered would be of utmost value to the Yavapai plan.

13

U Day Ah's successful escape was never far from the thoughts of Don Miguel Peralta as he was engineering the mining operation he had dreamed about for so long. He could not reconcile whether the girl would be a positive force in his plan or act as a destroyer of it. Because of her very existence, he did not know whether the Yavapai would attack his miners en masse or pull back to avoid the Mexican operation long enough for him to complete it and leave voluntarily.

Capitán Garces could not get U Day Ah out of his mind either. During the time she was with them, he had dreamed of an impossible relationship with her. He knew very well that there was never even a chance that she would choose a man like himself. Yet he had dreamed. Now, she was gone and a part of himself with her. He had no reason to think that he would ever see her again, so Capitán Garces doubled his efforts in his duties to make secure the Peralta expedition.

Manuel Peralta had all he could do now to keep a firm grip on the expedition's miners so that each facet of the operation would proceed smoothly. His thoughts occasionally drifted to U Day Ah, but realizing the futility of it, he went on about his work. Yet, futile or not, the thoughts of her would still occur.

Upon arriving at the site of the Ancient Ones, Don Miguel immediately had el capitán order guard patrols, two men to a patrol, to encircle the camp and give the alarm if necessary. El capitán had placed stationary guards on the tops of the hills surrounding the camp, except the hill containing the ruins of the Ancient Ones. Considering the efforts made, the camp seemed as secure as it could possibly have been, barring an actual stockade.

———

A little over a week had passed since their arrival, and the patrol was slowly making its rounds. Then the guard patrol saw the tracks: the tracks of two horses, which had been tied to brush some distance from the camp and had been ridden away also. They had ridden in from the northeast and ridden out the same way. The horses were not shod. The camp had been scouted by Indians, probably Yavapai. The guards split up, as per their orders, one staying with the tracks and the other riding to summon el capitán.

Capitán Garces and Manuel Peralta both rode out to see the tracks. They saw the footprints of two men also in the area. The men looked at each other, each thinking the same thing. The footprints showed that U Day Ah had not been there, but two warriors had been. The Yavapai knew for certain where the Peraltas were and why they were there. Having assessed the tracks, the guards were left to continue their patrol, and both Manuel and el capitán galloped to inform Don Miguel.

Don Miguel was not hard to find. He was standing, arms folded, directly in front of his tent awaiting their arrival. He had seen their hurried exit from camp. Realizing that something of importance caused it, he felt he should be informed also. Manuel and el capitán dismounted and, along with Don Miguel, entered his tent. Manuel was chosen to tell of the tracks and of the fact that the encampment had been discovered by the Yavapai.

Don Miguel let out a long sigh of relief. He had feared that the outlying miners may have been attacked. Evidently, the Yavapai had been on a fact-finding mission. Well, the Yavapai had done a good job. Now, Don Miguel knew that they had been discovered. He had been expecting it. It was no surprise. Unfortunately, it confirmed the fact that U Day Ah had not perished in her escape. She was alive and had informed the Yavapai of his presence and his motive. Now what? What will the Yavapai do?

The three sat quietly for some time in Don Miguel's tent, until Don Miguel said, "What has been done is done. Now we must be able to react to whatever comes next. I had hoped that U Day Ah had vanished without being able to alert the Yavapai. We would have been discovered eventually, but later would have been preferable. Had we been accidently discovered, we might have been able to convince the Yavapai that we were just a temporary visitor. We can be sure that U Day Ah has told her leaders everything she knew. Between the three of us, we made sure that she could not have missed much."

The two young men each shot a sheepish glance at the other at this undisguised jab by Don Miguel.

Manuel spoke up. "Father, I know that Capitán Garces will do everything he can to provide us with all the security possible. I will order that no miner approach or provoke any Yavapai seen watching us. Unless they mount an attack on the outlying mines, what can they do against us anyway? We must seem a formidable force to them."

"Very true," said Don Miguel. "But we do not know how strong they are. In the past, the Yavapai traveled only in small bands because of the supply of game on their land. However, their land covers a large area. Should they decide to drive us out, they would have to gather all the bands together. This would take time. If they still hate us enough from the past, they might do that. If time has dulled their memory of those times, if enough of the old ones have died, we may be able to use that to our advantage. At this time, I do not know."

"Then, Father," said Manuel, "if I may say, we must act as if we have no intention to harm the Yavapai. We must go about our business as if there is no reason for hostilities on their part. If contact is made with them, it must be at least cordial, if not openly friendly. Perhaps, this can buy us the time we need to mine what we came for and leave here. If, as you say, the Yavapai are playing for time also, that may delay hostilities until we can escape from here."

"Many years ago, tricking and then forcing the Yavapai to work at the mines seemed to be the way to accomplish our mission," began Don Miguel. "It was wrong, I know, but it did not seem so at the time. We regarded the Yavapai as mere savages, pagans in a world that must be all Christian. They revolted as we would have in similar circumstances. They fought hard. We have your cavalry now, Capitán. Yet, if they still hate us and come at us, they will give us all we can handle," he declared.

"However," continued the don, "your general plan makes sense to me, Manuel. Implement it. If we have to make changes as necessary, we will, but for now, I see no other rational way to move forward."

"Don Miguel," offered el capitán, "years ago against the Chiricahua Apache, we made use of civilians to make the Chiricahua believe we had more soldiers than we actually had. Some of our miners who work here at our base camp have been in the military. They could put on a uniform shirt, carry a weapon, and make the Yavapai think we are stronger than we are. It may be that we can convince the Yavapai to take advantage of our seemingly friendly overtures more willingly."

Manuel said, "Good idea, Capitán. I see now how you attained your rank."

"Very funny," returned el capitán.

Don Miguel added his voice to the idea. "A good idea must be implemented properly. The extra soldiers seen here in camp will free real soldiers to escort and patrol the outlying mines. They are our most vulnerable operations. I believe your Lieutenant DaVia could be put in charge of that operation. What do you say, Capitán?"

"If you request, Don Miguel, I shall order it," answered el capitán.

"I detect a negative tone, Capitán. Tell me," ordered Don Miguel.

"No, sir. Lieutenant Diego DaVia is very capable of directing that operation. In fact, he may be more than just capable," returned el capitán.

"Tell me," ordered the don.

"Lieutenant Diego DaVia was once capitán of dragoons in the fight against the Chiricahua Apache in northern Chihuahua. He led a morning raid against a numerically superior force of Apache in which he was wounded. He continued to lead the attack until the surviving Apache had fled into the nearby hills. His efforts were heroic according to his dragoons. Rather than being decorated, his superiors in Mexico City acted shocked at the severity of the operation. He was reduced in rank to lieutenant for being overzealous in his attack on that village," related el capitán.

"How do you appraise Lieutenant DaVia, Capitán?" asked Don Miguel.

"I regard him as an officer of the highest caliber," answered el capitán.

"Good. It just may be that we will need his abilities and his zealousness in the weeks and months to come. He has already shown that he is a man who can get things done. I am recalling his ropes and mules idea to take us up that damn sandy canyon. Enough said. Carry on, gentlemen," ordered Don Miguel.

Within minutes, el capitán heard the voice of Lieutenant Diego DaVia outside his tent.

"Lieutenant DaVia, reporting as ordered, sir."

"Enter, Lieutenant," commanded el capitán. "Sit down, please."

"Thank you, sir," was the reply.

"Lieutenant DaVia, you lucky bastard, you have been noticed by Don Miguel Peralta, himself," said el capitán with a grin on his face.

"Uh oh. What did I do this time?" asked the lieutenant.

"Oh, no, this is a good thing, Lieutenant," said el capitán. "Don Miguel Peralta thinks you should be in charge of a special operation."

El capitán could not help but grin at the quizzical reaction on Lieutenant DaVia's face. "And I agree with him. You are the man for the job."

Once again came that look.

"Relax, DaVia. We need someone to organize and ride herd on the mines and miners on the outer perimeter of this operation. We have been found by the Yavapai. We have no idea what will happen next. It has been decided that we will present a formidable look to the Yavapai but do nothing to provoke them. We are trying to buy as much time as possible, maybe get away with it completely, before we might have to fight our way out of here. Twenty years ago, the Yavapai hated us, and rightfully so. They drove Don Peralta and his miners clear back to southern Sonora." said Capitán Garces.

"Ride herd?" said Diego DaVia. "Who suggested that I was a candidate to ride herd?"

"I told you that you were lucky. Don Miguel himself brought up your name. You impressed him as a man who could get things done or something like that. Your idea with the ropes and mules did it," said el capitán, laughing.

"Me and my big mouth. Oh, I can do the job. Will I have any help on this?" DaVia asked.

"There will be at least one cavalryman assigned to guard one, maybe two mines depending upon how near they are to each other. You will be in complete charge of that. At no time is any miner to act in any way but a friendly manner if encountered by the Yavapai. No one—I repeat—no one must provoke the Yavapai into hostile action," explained Capitán Garces.

"But, what if . . ." started Lieutenant DaVia.

"If we are attacked, we must defend ourselves. Think of that only as a last resort," stated El Capitán Garces. "Understand?"

"Yes, sir," came the reply.

"Now," said el capitán.

Lieutenant Diego DaVia, born in Spain, descendant of the ancient nobility of northern Italy, had hoped to quietly end his military career in some nondescript position, settle back with a fat little chica, and retire to a small villa somewhere in Sonora. His Chiricahua Apache adventure in Chihuahua, his subsequent demotion, had seemed to ensure that the villa would indeed be small, but until he could retire, he had to play soldier a little bit more. When asked if he would assist in accompanying a wagon train expedition, he felt that would get him out of town for a while. Not a bad idea except that this happened to be the wagon train. And this was no traditional wagon train.

Oh, well. Lieutenant DaVia knew he was a soldier and a damned good one at that. He was an officer. On this mission, no one would ever say he did not perform as a professional.

Lieutenant DaVia wasted no time. He saddled his horse, loaded his few supplies, and headed out of the main camp to begin his visits to each of the outlying mines. He had no illusions. Anything could happen on this mission. Or maybe nothing would happen. No, something definitely will happen. So much for "lucky"!

It was a mile or so from the main camp to the first outlying mine. Riding his horse at a walk, he found himself thinking about his situation. He remembered his court martial for the incident in Chihuahua, Mexico. He had been a full capitán of dragoons, a military unit of light cavalry using not only pistols but lances. In a scarcely remembered skirmish with the Chiricahua Apache, he had learned a bitter lesson.

The Chiricahua warriors were not the tribe's only warriors. He had positioned his dragoons well in the mesquite and creosote foliage surrounding the Apache encampment. They were ready to charge when they were attacked from behind by warriors who had been concealed. They whirled to face the enemy. As they did so, a large force of mounted Apache attacked from the site of the encampment. Unable to charge in both directions, he ordered a full charge into the brush against the original group of warriors. His dragoons took some casualties, but in doing so, the Apache warriors lost many of their number also. Later, it was discovered that these original warriors from the brush were actually Apache women and young boys. This taking of lives, of women and young boys, was clearly against the policy of the dragoons as well as overall military policy.

Even though these Apache women and boys were attacking as if they were warriors, and Capitán Diego DaVia was in fact blameless for the outcome of the incident, the court martial penalized him for not being aware of his total surroundings prior to the attack. If he had been, the judges said, the attack would not have occurred. Therefore, the loss of these women and boys would not have occurred either. The court martial was implementing this sort of judgment in many matters regarding the Apache in order to placate them into settling back into a peaceful relationship with the Mexican local government. It did not work, but it did result in a reduction in rank for Capitán DaVia to Lieutenant DaVia.

Lieutenant DaVia's opinion of the whole matter, if vocalized, would turn the air green for miles around.

Lieutenant DaVia arrived at the first outlying mine. That was the first of many. As he arrived at each of them, he began issuing orders for the existing soldiers to begin irregular patrols to protect these miners. In a very short time, he had patrols crisscrossing to confuse the Yavapai as to where any patrol might be at any given time. It worked well for a long period of time. Lieutenant DaVia was content to oversee these arrangements on site, a process that kept him out of the main Peralta encampment most of the time.

14

Weeks went by. Don Miguel was very pleased that no confrontations had occurred with the Yavapai. However, the fact that Yavapai warriors had been watching the activities at the Peralta camp disturbed him greatly. No one else knew how worried he actually was. He had seen, first-hand, what could happen if these warriors attacked. It would not be pretty. But he was constantly being reassured by el capitán that his cavalry could handle any such move on the part of the Yavapai. After all, fifty mounted cavalry, all trained, battle-hardened professional soldiers, could surely outmatch undisciplined, primitive warriors. That sounded good—for a while. In the quiet hours of the night, however, his mind would go back to an earlier time. And it then took some time for the don to sleep.

———

Encounters in the outlying desert between Lieutenant DaVia and his patrols with Yavapai were occurring more frequently, always at a distance and always two warriors at a time. Each knew that they had been seen by the others, but no hostility was shown. El capitán briefed Manuel and Don Miguel after each occurrence. In each case, the opinion was that the Yavapai were monitoring what to them was an incursion into their land for an unknown purpose. As long as no one on either side made a hostile move, perhaps nothing would come of it. They all agreed that this was wishful thinking. They were in a situation that they knew not how to change. Clearly, the Yavapai had the first move.

The miners, to their credit, continued their work in spite of the obvious threat of attack. Existing mines were being located and reopened.

Don Miguel had spent a good deal of time with each mining team to locate the mines left behind many years earlier. After the Peraltas were driven from the mines, the Yavapai attempted to cover and disguise each location. They had done a good job; however, Don Miguel knew the locations of all these very profitable holes in the ground. Not being foolish, he also had made a journal. Each location had been mapped. Not even Don Miguel's sons had ever seen the journal. Even though the land had changed due to fire, flood, and foliage over the years, and a good deal of digging was involved, Don Miguel found every one of them.

Once covered or destroyed, in the mind of the Yavapai, the location of the mine was forgotten. All this had happened a full generation ago for the Yavapai. The young ones had never seen the mines. The old ones did not remember their locations. All that was known was that the mines had existed and that the Yavapai people had been forced to work them. The Yavapai were determined that this was never to happen again.

Each time a Yavapai was spotted, a runner was sent to summon Lieutenant DaVia. In most cases, as Lieutenant DaVia arrived, the Yavapai disappeared into the desert. Lieutenant DaVia was spending much time on horseback. Now and then he would have to return to the Peralta camp to resupply and rest. At these times, he would meet with Capitán Garces.

The two men had a great deal of respect for each other. Each had been tested in battle: both with the North Americans in the recent war and against the Apache in both Chihuahua and Sonora. The demotion of Lieutenant DaVia held little interest for Capitán Garces. El capitán knew, and had even consoled Lieutenant DaVia of the fact, that his demotion was a political one of a military wanting to pursue a pacification policy toward the Apache.

Lieutenant DaVia knew Capitán Garces as more than a spit and polish officer. Although he made a dashing figure in his cavalry officer uniform, he had gotten that uniform dirty, bloody, and torn in many battles with Mexico's enemies. He knew what was required and was not afraid to do it. When he gave an order, it was based on knowledge and experience. Both men knew that the other was able to accomplish any mission assigned to him, a political court martial notwithstanding.

Therefore, when Lieutenant DaVia stated that something was happening out in that desert, el capitán listened. Lieutenant DaVia was becoming very uneasy about the organized observation on the part of the Yavapai. He told el capitán, "These are not just curious warriors wanting to see what was happening. These warriors are performing as precise an intelligence-gathering operation as I've ever seen.

"Every time we see them, and turn to look back at them, they turn and disappear into the desert. They do not discuss it with each other; they just do it. They are acting under orders," asserted Lieutenant DaVia.

"Can you be sure?" asked el capitán.

"Oh, yes," replied the lieutenant. "We have thirty mines out there that we are actively working. We also have seen two Yavapai warriors placed out there for each of those mines. Each pair of Yavapai warriors is assigned to the same mine. They are out there every day."

"You are right, Lieutenant. This is not just the erratic behavior of a primitive people. This is a controlled effort to gain information on our daily operation," agreed Capitán Garces. "What would be their plan?"

"It's obvious, Capitán. They are biding their time. But they want to know exactly what our weak areas are. They will attack, but only when they are ready. I doubt that they are able to do it now. They are waiting for more warriors from someplace," said the lieutenant.

"Let's meet with Don Miguel," suggested el capitán. "He knows these people."

Don Miguel was very visible that day. He had been pacing back and forth in front of his tent. He had been more and more disturbed over the status quo with the Yavapai. He did not want an attack, of course, but he felt he did not know all that he needed to about what was happening. This, for a commander of a large operation, was disconcerting at best. He did not like it at all.

He also did not like living in a tent. He had given orders when they first began identifying the mines that a stone building be constructed near the closest mine. He wanted his headquarters moved out of the area below the Rock in the Shape of a Man's Head. There was a canyon running northwest from the current camp, at the end of which was the mine where Don Peralta had headquartered in years past. Don Miguel had ordered a stone building to house himself and the supply of processed gold prior to its transport back to Mexico. There was a spring for fresh water about fifty yards from the mine itself. The canyon was secluded and thought to be easily defendable. The building had not yet been completed. The don was not happy about that. Autumn had become winter some time ago. Cold weather had set in.

Therefore, Don Miguel was already in a less than happy mood when el capitán and Lieutenant DaVia approached him.

"Buenos tardes, gentlemen," said Don Miguel somewhat formally, indicating his current mood.

"Buenos tardes, Señor Don," came the reply.

"You have something on your minds," said the don. "What is it?"

"May we discuss this at a distance from the activities of the men?" asked el capitán. "And is Manuel available to join us?"

"Sergeant, fetch my son Manuel to us. He is in the wash behind the chuck wagon," ordered Don Miguel.

Manuel joined them, and they retired to the don's command tent. When all were seated, el capitán spoke. "Don Miguel, we have spent weeks patiently waiting after the Yavapai discovered us to see what they were going to do. The men, both your miners and my cavalry, are extremely nervous about it. The Yavapai stay out of musket range yet in full view of our men. The men continue to do their jobs, and that speaks well for their courage and their discipline regarding the order not to provoke the Yavapai. But this cannot last."

Lieutenant DaVia interrupted. "My roving guards are finding it to be more and more difficult to keep the miners calm. All are trying, sir, but something must be done."

"Manuel, what have you to report in this regard?" asked his father.

"I agree with Lieutenant DaVia, Father," answered Manuel. "This morning I myself was followed closely for about a mile by two Yavapai. They wore no paint but were close enough for me to see their faces. It took all my restraint not to set my horse to a run, either at them or away from them."

"Yes. I see," said the don. "And I agree. Something must be done before someone loses control. Caballeros, what do you suggest? Any ideas?"

After a long tension-filled minute, Manuel said, "Father, we must communicate with them in some way. Anything! Any way we do it is fine, just so long as we begin talking with them. If we are talking with them, maybe we won't have to be fighting with them—at least for a while."

"Years ago, we communicated with the Yavapai," began Don Miguel. "We fought with the Yavapai. We lied to the Yavapai. We subjugated the Yavapai and others. We forced them to work in our mines, just as the Spanish missionaries had before us. In the end, we were forced to run for our very lives," spoke Don Miguel.

"El Capitán, Lieutenant DaVia and I think that if we do not talk with them soon, we will be fighting them soon," said Manuel Peralta.

"Don Miguel," Lieutenant DaVia addressed him. "I have fought the Apache—often; I believe these Yavapai are no different. They recognize strength, fear, and insult. Sooner or later the fact that we are ignoring their presence will be seen as insulting to them. Their pride as warriors will be hurt. They will react violently to that. We need to meet with them."

"Caballeros," began the don, "I can see you have been paying attention. You have been watching this situation closely as have I, and I agree with you. We cannot gamble that nothing will happen if we do not start it. To delay contact with the Yavapai any longer would be foolish."

"How shall we initiate talks, Father?" asked Manuel Peralta.

"Tomorrow after breakfast, the four of us will ride slowly out of camp. We will ride together under a large white flag of truce. The Yavapai have seen it before, and they will recognize it as a sign of peace."

"You have dealt with the Yavapai before, Don Miguel," said Capitán Garces. "Do we dare leave the area with no senior officer in charge?"

"Sergeant Mendoza will keep order here," replied the don. "The Yavapai will not attack any location while we march under the white flag. After all, they recognize our officers by now. It will show more respect for them by all showing up."

"Don Miguel, we do not even know where the Yavapai are encamped," stated el capitán.

"From the look in your eyes, Don Miguel, I would say that you have a damn good idea where the Yavapai might be. Am I right?" asked Lieutenant DaVia.

"We will cross this wash and Camp Creek, then move northeast across the rolling desert to where the Rio Verde flows out of these mountains. I expect to find their camp there. Once the Yavapai scouts see us riding that way under the white flag, they will lead us to their camp," asserted Don Miguel.

"Caballeros, alert Sergeant Mendoza of his duties for tomorrow and make your own preparations. We leave after breakfast at dawn," ordered Don Miguel Peralta.

15

Nanni Chaddi awakened on that morning with an uneasiness he could not shake. He had slept well early on, but his dreams would not let him sleep the full night. The vision of whips, chains, and men straining to load quartz rocks filled with gold to the arrastras would not leave his mind. He had sat upright in his wikiup until dawn. At dawn's light, he settled down, opened the door flap, and stepped outside. The dawn was just allowing the red and golden light of day into the Yavapai camp. The morning was chilly with a light but occasionally brisk breeze.

He had spent many days in the small camp by the river. From here, he controlled the many scouting parties observing the miners and soldiers of the Peralta expedition. His scouts were eating their morning meal and preparing to resume their duties. The first face he saw was that of O hi Cama. The young warrior stood when he saw Nanni Chaddi.

"We have spent much time watching the miners," said O hi Cama.

"Too much time. Weeks have turned into moons," said Nanni Chaddi. "We know exactly what they are doing."

"Now we must decide how and when we will drive them out or kill them. Do we think the same?" asked O hi Cama.

"Yes," said Nanni Chaddi. "But we drove them away before—long ago. Yet now they have returned. The need for the yellow stones must be great in their world. If I could send them away permanently by giving them all the yellow stones in our land, I would."

"I would prefer to simply kill them all and be done with it," said O hi Cama.

"If we had hundreds of warriors like you, O hi Cama," said Nanni Chaddi, "I would attack today. But not all warriors are like you. There- fore, we must wait until we have enough warriors."

"I fear we do not have enough time, my chieftain," said O hi Cama. "I fear the intruders are getting nervous and fearful seeing our warriors watching them. We may be forcing them to do something stupid—like attack us."

"We cannot let that happen. Not yet," said Nanni Chaddi. "We are not ready."

O hi Cama decided to press the issue. "We both have been thinking of nothing else since the miners' return. We both know that we need more and better armed warriors. But you have not told me from where and how we will obtain them."

Nanni Chaddi replied, "You have waited patiently, and you are my right hand in this, O hi Cama. We wait for the Apache."

"The Apache!" exclaimed O hi Cama. "Why would the Apache help us?"

"The Apache have fought the Mexicans for generations. For months the Chiricahua and the Mescalero have been fighting in the south. Many warriors are fighting that fight. The Mexicans seem to be getting pushed farther south. The Apache are claiming great victories," answered Nanni Chaddi.

"If this is true, how did a Mexican force of miners and soldiers man- age to make their way here—so far to their north?" questioned O hi Cama.

"Their runner informed me that their scouts thought these miners were going to the place called California in the far west. That is until they turned north toward us. Then it was too late to pull warriors from the other war to kill them. I am told the fighting in Chihuahua is still going on. The Mexicans do not surrender to the Apache easily," answered Nanni Chaddi.

"Nor would I! But you say we must wait for the Apache to defeat the Mexicans before we can drive these miners from our land?" asked O hi Cama incredulously. "Surely we can muster enough to kill these intruders!"

"If these intruders were just untrained miners or even just soldiers, but they are not. They are the same people who enslaved us years ago. They know who we are. They know our warriors. Yet they have come anyway. They are being wary, but their leaders seem to be without fear of us," stated Nanni Chaddi. "We must be cunning. We must wait. We must buy time until our Apache brothers can help us."

"We must make them think that we have forgotten? We must make them think that we wish only a strong peace with them? How can we do that?" asked O hi Cama. "We do not even speak their language."

Calmly and quietly Nanni Chaddi said, "We have U Day Ah."

"This is how we fight our enemies—using our women?" shouted O hi Cama.

"Calm yourself," said Nanni Chaddi firmly. "Sit down. You will live your name, O hi Cama: 'Striking the Enemy.' But, for now, we will plan to meet with these Mexicans. We will be friendly toward them in order to lower the risk of a fight and buy time for us to become strong enough to kill them," stated Nanni Chaddi.

"I will bring her here," said O hi Cama.

U Day Ah was still having her breakfast when O hi Cama strode across the camp directly to her wikiup. She saw him coming and rose to await him. They stood facing each other for just a moment.

"You have purpose to come to me this early," stated U Day Ah.

"Yes," returned O hi Cama. "It seems our people need you."

"More than O hi Cama needs me?" chided U Day Ah.

"We have not spoken of such things before and must not now," said O hi Cama.

"Are you saying that the time will come when we will speak of such things?" prodded U Day Ah.

"You are a very outspoken young woman. You should not be so," stated O hi Cama.

"Yesterday you thought of me as a mere girl. Now, I am an outspoken woman," teased U Day Ah. "What has changed?"

"You are about to become a warrior for your people," said O hi Cama.

"A what!?" exclaimed U Day Ah.

"Nanni Chaddi will explain," said O hi Cama, fearful that his face would tell all about his feeling for her.

Gently, as she looked up at him incredulously, he led her to Nanni Chaddi.

U Day Ah could not believe her ears as Nanni Chaddi and O hi Cama explained their plans for her. She was to use her experience with the Mexicans and her womanly charm to convince the Mexicans that the Yavapai were intent on a peaceful relationship with them. She was to be a very personable interpreter for any discussions between the Yavapai and the Peraltas. In that capacity, she would make the image of peace much more effectively than would Yavapai warriors.

She voiced her objections noisily and violently to both Nanni Chaddi and O hi Cama but to no avail. The decision was made. She would do it. The next morning, dressed to impress, she accompanied O hi Cama and two other warriors as they left the Yavapai camp. The women of the tribe had made her a very special dress of soft doeskin. It was embroidered in colorful beads and turquoise. Matching high-top doeskin moccasins and turquoise beads made a very beautiful impression. Her long, shining, raven-black hair banded with turquoise, U Day Ah looked incredibly beautiful as they rode south across the rolling desert toward the Peralta camp.

O hi Cama, along with two other Yavapai warriors, were dressed in their finest clothing and headdresses. They wore no paint but tied their hair with deerskin bands, eagle feathers, and turquoise beads. They were unarmed, save for their knives and the traditional short lances. There was a small ravine that the four had to cross as they traversed the rolling desert. At the earliest opportunity, they urged their horses up the embankment. No sooner had they reached the crest emerging onto the flat desert floor when they had to rein in their mounts. Had they not done so, they would have collided with the Peralta delegation. The horses plunged violently, frightened at the suddenness of the meeting.

Don Miguel, leading the Peralta delegation, was nearly unseated as his horse reared backward at the near collision. Manuel Peralta, Capitán Garces, and Lieutenant DaVia gained control of their mounts as the dust swirled around them. Out of the swirling dust and the confusion came the realization to all that the meeting they had all intended for later in the day had just occurred. The Yavapai warriors, clutching their lances, looked fiercely upon the Peraltas. The Peraltas looked likewise at the warriors. At any second the feared war could begin.

Then, U Day Ah moved her horse a few feet forward, recognized Manuel Peralta and Capitán Garces, and smiled. The result was entirely predictable. The men recognized her and smiled their delight. The immediate tension was broken. Don Miguel Peralta and O hi Cama did not smile. They looked into each other's face as two warrior adversaries and took measure of the other. They were not disappointed. Each readily saw the worth of the other.

But the smiles and the release of tensions were contagious. Another moment elapsed before words were spoken. Don Miguel spoke first. "U Day Ah, we are so glad to see that you are safe and well. You left us without a word, so we were all very worried about you." As he spoke, Don Miguel made a wide gesture with his hand to include Manuel and el capitán as also very concerned about her. Both young men were very pleased at seeing U Day Ah again. They were taking much pleasure seeing her so resplendently beautiful in her finery and astride her paint pony.

O hi Cama recognized the young men's pleasure at seeing U Day Ah and was not happy about it. He was dedicated to the plan to be friendly to these people, but he did not like it at all. Now sensing the relationship, albeit wishful, on the part of the young Mexicans, he hated the whole idea. He recognized his jealousy for what it was and determined that he would put it aside. But not forever.

U Day Ah motioned O hi Cama forward. At that point, wishing to be in control of this meeting, Don Peralta began the introductions. As each was recognized in turn, each merely nodded to the rest of the group. U Day Ah did likewise also. After another interminable period of silence, U Day Ah surprised everyone by inviting the Peralta party to the Yavapai camp to meet Nanni Chaddi. One of the warriors was dispatched to ride ahead to prepare the camp and Nanni Chaddi.

Don Peralta had been prepared to ride up to the Yavapai camp and surprise the Yavapai with his own brand of diplomacy. However, U Day Ah seemed to have stolen his thunder by taking the initiative from him. Now who was actually in control of this diplomatic operation? At any rate, he put on the mantle of the elder statesman and rode at U Day Ah's side to the Yavapai camp.

The messenger, riding at top speed, was able to give the camp about half an hour to prepare for the Peraltas. Nanni Chaddi barely had time to change into his warrior chieftain finery. But he was every bit the image of a great chieftain in bright feathers, deerskin, and turquoise. To add to his purpose as a welcoming statesman, Nanni Chaddi, along with two more warriors, awaited the arrival of the Peraltas mounted on horseback, at the edge of the encampment.

Within a few moments of the Yavapai's' preparation, the Peralta party arrived. O hi Cama and U Day Ah escorted Don Miguel Peralta ahead to meet Nanni Chaddi. Manuel Peralta, Capitán Garces, and Lieutenant DaVia, as per protocol in these matters, remained mounted behind at attention. U Day Ah introduced Nanni Chaddi to Don Miguel Peralta as "chieftain of the Rio Verde Yavapai." Don Miguel was introduced as "chieftain of the Mexican miners." Both rode their horses toward the other and clasped hands in greeting. Each man's eyes took in the other man's stature instantly. The look of a leader of men was recognizable to each. Both men smiled their appreciation of the moment and each other.

Don Miguel understood only very little of the Yavapai language. Nanni Chaddi understood none of the Spanish language. U Day Ah conveyed each man's greeting to the other. Through U Day Ah, Nanni Chaddi invited the Peraltas to dismount and take shade under the central ramada. Refreshments of fruit and juice were offered and accepted. Small talk followed in advance of discussing any real issues. Don Miguel broke the ice by stating: "U Day Ah is a fine representative of your nation. Although she has suffered much in her young life, she has shown the resiliency of her people in her courage and ability to make her way to her home. She has impressed all in our entire expedition."

Nanni Chaddi replied: "U Day Ah has shown a Yavapai warrior's heart in the form of a woman. We have great pride in her."

U Day Ah blushed as she was asked to repeat these words of her own praise.

"It pleased us all greatly that after we found her wounded and suffering, we were able to help her regain her health," said Don Miguel. "She is a brave young woman."

Nanni Chaddi nodded his agreement.

"The only thing that concerned all of us was that she chose to leave us so soon," said Don Miguel.

"I do not understand," said Nanni Chaddi. "She had every right to seek her own people."

"Yes, she did," agreed Don Miguel. "And it was understandable to all of us. However, we had planned to seek out her people and return her safely to the Yavapai soon after we arrived at our destination. Her sudden early departure worried us greatly."

"Your concern for the well-being of one of our people is well taken," said Nanni Chaddi through U Day Ah.

Then Nanni Chaddi added, "Such concern for any of the Yavapai people is something we have not experienced in the past. It is sad to remember the conflicts that occurred in my youth."

"It saddens me also, Nanni Chaddi," said Don Miguel Peralta. "You were very young; I was older but still young enough to make foolish decisions. I make no excuse. I was wrong. Time and life have proven that to be true."

"I remember only what I saw as a child. I believe that life breeds fools in everything that happens," stated Nanni Chaddi. "But what now, Don Peralta?"

"What now?" asked Don Miguel. "What do you mean, Nanni Chaddi?"

U Day Ah was careful to choose her words, as this conversation was beginning to discuss serious subjects. U Day Ah interpreted Nanni Chaddi's words: "What is your reason for returning to these holes you made in the past? Why are you here?"

"U Day Ah, please interpret my words so that there can be no misunderstanding of them," said Don Miguel Peralta. "I am getting old. The world, as I had known it, is changing, and I can do nothing about it. Before I die, I wish to take back to my home country as much of the yellow stones as I can, for my family and my country, so that I will have left them all that I can."

"Why should the Yavapai allow this to happen after what had happened to us before?" asked Nanni Chaddi. As he spoke, he leaned slightly forward to be sure his eyes conveyed the meaning of his words.

"I would make this peace to you. I will be here only about one year more. Before I leave, I will return the Earth close to the way I found it. I will make every effort to leave no scars on the land. I will keep the Rock in the Shape of a Man's Head sacred. I will not allow anyone to enter the homes of the Ancient Ones. I will not harm any Yavapai. I will do these things out of respect for the Yavapai, for the memory of mistakes made in the past, and for you, Nanni Chaddi, chieftain of the Rio Verde Yavapai," vowed Don Miguel Peralta.

"How do you pledge this, Chief Peralta?" asked Nanni Chaddi.

"I pledge this with my words, spoken from my heart, eye to eye, one man to another. And I further vow that, after I return to my country, I will tell of the Yavapai, of their wisdom, their strength, and their greatness as a people," said Don Miguel Peralta.

"You promise to be a grateful guest in my land, Chief Peralta. However, you are an uninvited guest. You visit this place even after the sadness of your last visit. Your words promise a peaceful visit, yet the Yavapai receive nothing that we do not already have or can readily take," said Nanni Chaddi. "You are a bold man, Chief Peralta."

"I have come from too far away over trails too difficult to be able to offer you presents to buy your friendship. Such things, from the character I see in your eyes, would have been judged as insulting by you. I choose to address you man to man, chieftain to chieftain, to offer you a friendly, danger-free relationship as equals in the hope that we both agree that the past is now dead, as dead as those from both our peoples who perished in that hated fight," asserted Don Peralta.

"The memory of that bad time is still in the hearts of the Yavapai. But you come here, bravely into our village, to speak directly to us as a man should. You are promising only to take the yellow stones and, peacefully, leave. You promise to keep the homes of the Ancient Ones sacred. But hear me! New holes in the Earth Mother will not be tolerated! We will give this promise time to work. Understand, Chief Peralta, the Yavapai will not violate this agreement. We will see if your people can abide by their own promises," bluntly stated Nanni Chaddi.

The unspoken part of that statement was very clear to all Peraltas hearing the words of Nanni Chaddi. Any violation of the peace would be cause for attack by the Yavapai.

The two leaders of their people stood and faced each other. Each clasped the outstretched hand of the other firmly. An agreement had been made. If the agreement could be upheld, all would be well. If not . . . ?

Before the Peralta delegation took their leave, Don Peralta invited Nanni Chaddi, O hi Cama, and all who wished to visit the Peralta camp. Of course, U Day Ah must accompany them. As they rode away from the Yavapai camp, they could not help but feel the burning gaze of O hi Cama.

16

It was getting late. The meeting had lasted well into the time when an evening meal would have been served. The offer of food was not made. The omission was duly noted by all the Peraltas. They were hungry. The sun had set some time ago, but they continued the ride toward their main camp. They rode in silence. Shortly before the riders neared the most outlying of the mines, they entered a fairly wide wash protected by low embankments on either side. Here, Don Miguel Peralta called a halt.

All dismounted and stretched their legs. Riding over that rolling desert terrain was no picnic. Low groans were heard as they stretched their muscles. "Caballeros, we need to talk," said the don. "What are your thoughts after what you have just seen and heard?"

Manuel Peralta spoke first. "All things considered, I thought it went well. No one was shot. No one was shouting. Did you ever see anything like U Day Ah?"

El capitán took his turn. "I never have. My God, she looked beautiful! Are we sure she is just in her teen years? She seemed to be in complete control as she translated the whole meeting. U Day Ah may have kept those two warriors calm enough to think clearly about keeping the peace."

"U Day Ah may have turned out to be the key to how long we can work these mines. Many good words were spoken today. The chief, Nanni Chaddi, seemed to mean what he said. I hope those words can be trusted, and we can get our work done and get out of here without a fight. It is too soon to tell," said Don Miguel.

"Nanni Chaddi was lying through his teeth!" exclaimed Lieutenant DaVia. "The only thing you can trust from his mouth was that they are not in any position to attack us . . . yet. I don't give a damn what was spoken by that Nanni Chaddi. I was watching the eyes of that tall warrior beside him. If those eyes could kill, all by themselves, we'd all be dead and roasted by now."

"Lieutenant DaVia, speak a little louder. All of Sonora did not hear you!" voiced el capitán.

"All right, I'll speak softly. But it changes nothing. That warrior is at war with us right now. I've seen that look from Apaches ready to take on my dragoons," reiterated Lieutenant DaVia.

"I, too, have seen that look, Lieutenant," agreed Don Miguel. "But the words of their chieftain must be honored. I expect Nanni Chaddi to keep his word and hold his warriors in check."

"Don Miguel, I hope we are not going to let these visitors see anything they can use against us," stated Lieutenant DaVia. "Our weaknesses are popping up all over the place."

"We are not going to let down our guard, are we, Capitán?" asked the don. "But we are going to milk this agreement for all we can get out of it. Time is what we need. Time to fill the leather sacks with the gold we came for."

Manuel and el capitán were uncharacteristically silent during this conversation between Don Miguel and Lieutenant DaVia. They were simply allowing him to voice their opinion for them. He was overlooking nothing.

"I believe the Yavapai are stalling for time, too," said DaVia. "They do not have the manpower to kick us out . . . yet. But what happens when their reinforcements arrive?"

"We play nice with them until we can no longer. Or we make a run for Sonora, hopefully with all our gold," said Don Miguel. "Spring has begun, and the weather will soon become too hot to fight a war. We will use that summertime. We will suffer the heat, but we will be ready in the autumn."

"We'll be nice all spring and summer, but in the autumn, we'd damn well better be gone!" asserted Lieutenant DaVia, with all heads nodding approval.

With that, the Peralta delegation headed for the main camp.

17

The last orange and purple glow of sunset still showed in the Rio Verde camp of the Yavapai. The glow illuminated the faces of Nanni Chaddi, O hi Cama, and U Day Ah as they watched the Peralta delegation disappear in the distance. A strained silence prevailed for a few moments. Then, in a voice straining, but failing, to sound calm: "Did we just promise to be friendly and peaceful to these intruders?" rasped O hi Cama.

"Yes," said U Day Ah.

"But we now are bound by our word to these people!" protested O hi Cama.

"Would you have us do otherwise?" asked Nanni Chaddi.

"But you have given them all they came for! You ask nothing of them in return," argued O hi Cama. "These are the same people who enslaved our people—and worse!"

Nanni Chaddi turned, looked at both O hi Cama and U Day Ah, and said in a low, calm tone, "They are the same people. Their chief was as old as I now am when he came here in the past. He made the same mistakes as those who came before him, but even so there is no forgiveness in my heart for what he did to the Yavapai."

"Then surely we must not just give them all they want," argued O hi Cama.

"This Chief Peralta wisely gave in to demands I was about to make, before I made them," returned Nanni Chaddi. "Would you have me start a war now when we have nowhere near enough warriors to do it? We have no workable plan to win such a war. The Yavapai would lose many brave warriors for nothing. You have seen. These men are mostly soldiers, well mounted and armed. They do not have their women and children here as we do. Starting such a war would be unwinnable for us. No. We must gain time to draw warriors from our friends."

"He promised only to protect the Rock in the Shape of a Man's Head and the homes of the Ancient Ones," said O hi Cama.

"Yes," said Nanni Chaddi. "I believe he will do that because of the trouble it caused last time, when they showed no respect for the Ancient Ones."

"But Nanni Chaddi," interrupted O hi Cama, "what about opening new holes in Mother Earth for the yellow stones?"

"U Day Ah, do you understand about the new holes?" asked Nanni Chaddi.

"After a time, they will not be able to stop themselves," said U Day Ah. "Their greed for the stones will force them to break their promise to you. And that will give the Yavapai the way to bring warriors to drive out the defilers of Earth Mother."

Another moment of silence ensued. O hi Cama had been looking deeply into the eyes of U Day Ah as she was speaking. When he spoke, his voice was calm and controlled. As if Nanni Chaddi was not even there, he said to U Day Ah, "You are wise beyond your years and wise also beyond other young women."

U Day Ah was stunned. She certainly did not expect such a compliment from such a warrior.

Nanni Chaddi remained silent. He noted, with pleasure, the admiration of U Day Ah by O hi Cama. Now, if he could only keep O hi Cama under control, the Yavapai could look forward to a fine future, but for now, plans must be made. "The day has lasted long. We must meet after the morning meal to discuss what we will do. U Day Ah, plan to join us."

U Day Ah did not look at Nanni Chaddi as he spoke this invitation. She looked at O hi Cama and was not disappointed. In his gaze she saw admiration. U Day Ah blushed. Her walk back to her wikiup was deliberately steady. She did not want to show her emotion at the invitation to the planning meeting or her excitement at the admiration of her by O hi Cama. She would enjoy a very satisfying rest that night.

Morning brought the three, joined by two other subchiefs, together in the council tent of Nanni Chaddi. Nanni Chaddi did not hesitate to bring the subchiefs up to date on what had been promised and later discussed. The subchiefs were not from the local area near the Peralta camp. Although sympathetic to the cause of ridding themselves of these Mexican intruders, remembering the former battle and the many casualties suffered, they were not eager to join another such battle soon. Because of the fact that, for the time in question, no battle was planned, they steadfastly supported the waiting plan of Nanni Chaddi.

All agreed that the plan, advanced by Nanni Chaddi and O hi Cama, was the only way they could hope to remove the Peraltas. However, the subchiefs did not like the fact that one of their young women, beautiful and fluent in Spanish as she was, should be so important to the plan that they agreed to follow. "This is work for warriors, not women," they argued. Not wanting to anger these subchiefs at this point, Nanni Chaddi sat in silence. U Day Ah endured what seemed to be an interminable period of silence.

Then, standing to his full height, his jaw set in an uncompromising manner, O hi Cama said, "Among the Yavapai, U Day Ah is not just a young woman. She has already earned the name Warrior Woman! I, O hi Cama, honor her above all Yavapai women. I have spoken."

Noting the set of O hi Cama's jaw, the low tone of his voice, and the piercing look in his eyes, the subchiefs could only murmur their approval. U Day Ah, Warrior Woman, stood, acknowledged their approval, and for the first time in her young life felt love for a young man. The look she gave him told O hi Cama that he had never done anything so right in his whole life.

The subchiefs rose, made their farewells, and left to rejoin their respective bands. They would be sure to repeat the story of the young girl, U Day Ah, now to be known as Warrior Woman. Nanni Chaddi, as the subchiefs left, turned and said, "I was swimming in quicksand over how I would sway the subchiefs about U Day Ah. Then, O hi Cama, you stood and proclaimed that U Day Ah was now Warrior Woman and showed why you will be known as my war chief over all others."

"U Day Ah is Warrior Woman. She has proven it by having survived what would have killed a lesser warrior. She has shown her courage by joining us in what we are doing against the Peraltas. Her intelligence has been proven by her ideas to make us successful," argued O hi Cama.

"Your naming Warrior Woman swayed the subchiefs," said Nanni Chaddi. "And you are right. U Day Ah is Warrior Woman."

"Stand, Warrior Woman," ordered Nanni Chaddi. "Among us, and among the Yavapai, you are Warrior Woman, but in our contact with the Mexican miners, you must retain the name U Day Ah. The name Warrior Woman will make them think in ways that we do not want. Do you understand?"

"Yes, my chief," said Warrior Woman.

Pride shown in the eyes of all—Nanni Chaddi, O hi Cama, and Warrior Woman.

The three Yavapai sat down to decide on the schedule of friendly delay to buy time against the Peraltas. "Spring has begun, and soon the full heat of summer will be upon us. No one in his right mind would want to fight a war in the heat of our summer. We must delay any confrontation with them until the cool wind makes the leaves fall. How shall we do this?" asked Nanni Chaddi.

Warrior Woman, without hesitation said, "O hi Cama and I will make frequent visits to their camp."

O hi Cama stood and, throwing his hands in the air, spinning around, his eyes wide open, asked, "Why don't we do something extremely dangerous, like go into the enemy camp? Warrior Woman, you are well named."

Warrior Woman smiled her incredible smile. "We have no choice."

"I know," said O hi Cama. "I know."

Nanni Chaddi decided to make his point in this matter. "There is one thing. I will not go to their camp. Warrior Woman, accompanied by a Yavapai warrior of the status of O hi Cama, will show respectful friendly intentions. But the possibility of your chieftain becoming a captive in their camp cannot be risked."

"Agreed," said both O hi Cama and Warrior Woman.

"You will wait one week, then begin the visits," said Nanni Chaddi.

18

Springtime in Sonora, Mexico . . . probably the most wondrous time of the year. The weather was balmy. The flowers were in bloom and filled the air with intoxicating fragrances. The people of Cananea were planting crops. Even the war with the Apache in nearby Chihuahua province was winding down.

Don Enrique Vasquez, alcalde of Cananea, had been enjoying every minute of this beautiful spring. His only concern was for his friend Don Miguel Peralta, who was on a mission of unknown danger. He had heard nothing from Don Miguel's expedition for months. Yaqui Indians had provided him with second-hand information, primarily from Mexicans/ Apaches, for a few weeks, noting that the expedition had been seen in the area of the Rio Salado. Enrique Vasquez had no idea where the Rio Salado flowed.

He had, in the months that had elapsed since Don Miguel was in Cananea, paid a few visits to the Peralta rancheria in Arizpe. The Peralta family welcomed him and pressed him for whatever news he might have for them. He could usually tell them very little. Today he would learn something. He paid the Peraltas a very casual visit this day. Pedro and Ramón met him with some concern showing in their faces.

"Don Enrique, is there any way we can contact my father?" asked Pedro.

"Why? Have you heard something?" returned Enrique.

"A courier has arrived from our holdings in California. The Americans in that area are putting great pressure on the Mexican landowners regarding their property rights. The old Spanish grants are being disputed. The attorneys are demanding the primary person named in the property rights appear in their courts," explained Pedro.

Don Enrique said, "This will require some thought . . . and some wine."

"Forgive me, Don Enrique. Ramón, tell my wife to bring wine," ordered Pedro Peralta.

"Don Enrique, do you think that my father has heard the news of El Presidente Santa Anna?" asked Pedro.

"I do not see how," said Don Enrique. "I have sent no word to him. I would not know how to reach him. I also did not think it would change his plans at all, so I did not bother."

"My father must be told. It may greatly affect his stay in the North," said Pedro. "The fact that El Presidente Santa Anna has been stripped of power and is living in exile somewhere outside of Mexico may negatively affect his plans. I believe Santa Anna was involved in this project somehow."

"Then Don Miguel must be made aware of this. I did not know before, or I would have tried to notify him anyway. The only way is to send a courier to find him. The dispatch papers must contain all information he will need relative to the problem in California. You can provide that of course," said Don Enrique. "I will have to find a way to get it to your father."

"What else do you need from us?" asked Pedro.

"Any information you can provide as to where you think the Sombrero Mines are will get us to where we might find him," said Don Enrique.

Pedro responded, "I have no idea other than it is about three hundred miles north of here."

A prolonged silence prevailed before Ramón said, "Pedro, remember the packet Father brought back from his meeting with el presidente? There may be a map or something in it."

"Get it," ordered Don Enrique.

Within a few minutes, Ramón returned wearing a big smile. "Look at all these drawings," he said.

It took no time at all to settle on the diagram, not really a map, that showed a fairly good route to be followed by the Peralta expedition to the Sombrero Mines. Theoretically, it could be followed. At least it would get them into the general area of the Sombrero Mines.

"I now need to find a guide to get your courier to your father," said Enrique Vasquez.

"No," said Ramón. "I am the courier. You find an Indian tracker to go with me."

Pedro not surprisingly disagreed. Don Enrique strenuously objected. However, Ramón said, "Who else can be trusted? No one. Therefore, I will go."

Don Enrique Vasquez, knowing that time was of the essence, did not delay. "Ramón, make ready. Tomorrow, you will accompany me to Cananea. One of my most trusted guards, a half Yaqui, will be your tracker. I would trust him with the lives of my family. We will give him a day to prepare, and then the two of you will depart for the Sombrero Mines and your father."

"Thank you, Don Enrique," said Ramón.

"Do either of you know what the hell you are doing?" questioned Pedro.

"Someone has to stay home with your wife, Pedro," said Ramón. "Would you prefer to go and let me stay with her?"

"Sometimes!" retorted Pedro.

Don Enrique Vasquez said, "I only wish I could go."

With that, all set about making the preparations for a long ride.

———

Very late the next day, after a strenuous ride, Don Enrique and Ramón Peralta arrived in Cananea. Immediately, Don Enrique sent for the Yaqui known as Emiliano. Emiliano smiled broadly when he was informed of his mission. He had no family, and he also had no fear. He had been performing his duties as guard for Don Enrique Vasquez for a few years. He was very good at his duties, but he found it to be boring. He longed for some action . . . anything! Emiliano loved the whole idea.

Ramón, although determined to successfully reach his father because of the importance of his mission, was as delighted as Emiliano to be off on this adventure. Emiliano was but a couple years older than Ramón, but it made no difference. They would get along very well.

The two couriers left early the next morning. They followed the diagram left by Don Miguel and proceeded with haste. They were not encumbered by wagons or a herd of mules. They each had a swift horse, and each led a pack mule. The only material carried was food, ammunition, and a few camp necessities. They were travelling light, and fast.

Neither Ramón nor Emiliano doubted that they would be able to follow Don Miguel's trail. Once in the Rio San Pedro Valley, an expedition of that size would leave many signs. This proved to be true. All they had to fear was just . . . the Apache.

19

Don Miguel Peralta, on his return to his base camp, made hurried preparations to receive his Yavapai guests whenever they would decide to visit. The camp was put in fine military order. Nothing was left out of its assigned place. Fortifications were strengthened, not to overtly suggest that a fight was imminent, but merely to show a high level of organization. Those men remaining and performing duties in camp were clean, neat, and well kempt. Don Miguel wished to impress the Yavapai with not only his openness, but his ability to handle any situation.

Sometime earlier, the stone cabin and warehouse he had ordered built had been completed, and he had moved into it. The location was approximately three-quarters of a mile northwest of the main camp. It was situated almost to the end of the canyon near the mine that had produced so well in the past. Above the cabin, a vertical shaft followed downward the vein of gold-laden quartz that had made the site a favorite of Don Miguel's. Around the base of the hillside, to the northwest of the cabin, a horizontal shaft had been dug to intercept the vein from below. Barely across the canyon floor from the horizontal shaft, an arrastra constructed years earlier by the Spanish was in full operation. This arrastra was used to separate the gold from the quartz rock in which it was imbedded.

Here, Don Miguel Peralta and Manuel Peralta made their headquarters. Capitán Garces preferred to camp with his cavalrymen. One room housed the two Peraltas. The other room was being used as a warehouse to store the processed gold. Here, the gold dust and nuggets were packed

The Arrastra

into leather bags for eventual shipment back to Mexico via mule packs. The miners, nearby and outlying, delivered their gold to the warehouse. As early as it was in the spring of the year, the warehouse was filling up with gold.

It would not be too long before there was enough gold to make the journey home. Don Peralta was beginning to think that there would be all that could be carried by mule as early as mid-autumn. He was allowing himself to think that perhaps a second expedition might be possible. Then, the thought of the Yavapai would bring him back to reality. Realistically, getting out of here alive with the gold would have to satisfy him and, of course, el presidente.

———

Precisely one week after having met with Nanni Chaddi, scouts reported that two Yavapai were slowly making their way toward the Peralta camp. It was reported that they were one warrior and one woman. Don Peralta summoned Manuel and hastened to the main camp. There, the Peraltas met with Capitán Garces to await the arrival of their Yavapai guests. None of the three members of the Peralta group knew which Yavapai were coming, but surely U Day Ah had to be one of them.

They were right. It was well past midday when U Day Ah entered a Peralta camp for the first time since her escape. She was inwardly very nervous but tried not to show it. Don Miguel did not really expect Nanni Chaddi to risk capture by coming, and he was right. O hi Cama followed U Day Ah into camp. Both Yavapai were dressed to impress in all their deerskin finery. Obvious to all, O hi Cama carried his lance but wore no paint. This outwardly was a friendly visit in response to an invitation.

Well before their arrival, two tents had been prepared for the possibility of honored guests. They were fitted with all the amenities thought necessary and comfortable for the expected Yavapai. Cots fitted with straw-filled mattresses, albeit homemade, plus crude but comfortable chairs were placed inside. All this was done on the chance that the guests would need to spend one or multiple nights in the Peralta camp.

After the scout first sighted the Yavapai, Don Miguel ordered that Manuel, Capitán Garces, and Lieutenant DaVia be present with the don to greet them. As an afterthought, Sergeant Mendoza was also requested to join the welcoming party. Don Miguel and Manuel Peralta were mounted and escorted the two guests into the encampment. Once in front of the welcoming tent, all dismounted and greeted each other with handshakes and smiles.

Noticeably, O hi Cama was the only one not smiling. His demeanor was a bit aloof from the outward celebration. He would evidently wait and see how friendly his hosts would be. But U Day Ah was all smiles. She greeted each of the men whom she had known before her escape with a smile and handshake. Her greeting of Don Miguel was respectful, openly friendly, yet reserved. She greeted Manuel and Capitán Garces in the same manner. U Day Ah had no previous relationship with Lieutenant DaVia. Her greeting to Lieutenant DaVia was a bit more formal. She sensed something in his look, however, that told her he could be very dangerous.

Sergeant Mendoza was another matter. She greeted him warmly, holding his hand for a full minute and speaking words of greeting. The sergeant told her how pleased he was that his young patient had improved so well and looked so beautiful. She responded by stating that, without his tender care, she would be dead.

O hi Cama understood the formal greetings and response with Don Miguel. After all, he was the Peralta chieftain. However, he recognized immediately the looks given to U Day Ah by el capitán and Manuel. He did not like those looks, not even a little bit. He, like U Day Ah, recognized the potential danger lurking within Lieutenant DaVia. The others were merely the ranking members of the delegation; Lieutenant DaVia struck O hi Cama as the warrior. He made a mental note to watch Lieutenant DaVia closely.

The warm greeting exchanged between U Day Ah and Sergeant Mendoza was understood for what it was by O hi Cama. In all probability, even a party of intruding Mexican miners could have one decent human being in their midst.

Thus began the visit. The guests were shown their accommodations and allowed to freshen up before touring the camp. The shadows were long before the Yavapai left their tents to walk around the encampment. The contrasts between shadow and bright desert rocks and vegetation seemed to symbolize the whole aspect of this visit. Standing out in stark relief, casting a long shadow across the encampment and wash beyond, the Rock in the Shape of a Man's Head seemed to stand guard over the entire valley.

In the shadow of the Rock in the Shape of a Man's Head, the Yavapai were escorted by both Manuel Peralta and Capitán Garces. The tension between these young men and O hi Cama was so thick, no one ventured a comment. O hi Cama made his face a mask to conceal his jealousy regarding U Day Ah and these Mexicans.

The evening meal was less formal than would have been the case with any other invited guests. Although very important guests, these were not trained in what would be called European protocol. Therefore, something comparable to a picnic atmosphere prevailed. All were seated on rough-cut benches, eating from metal plates. The camp cook did an admirable job preparing deer meat and various other fare from the camp's supplies. Entertainment was provided by one of the cavalrymen softly playing Mexican ballads on his Spanish guitar.

However, the Yavapai had had a long, hot ride through difficult trailless desert and were very tired. O hi Cama and U Day Ah graciously retired to their respective tents. Both realized the importance of this visit. The fact that they were expected by Nanni Chaddi to present an image of friendly, neighborly interest in the operation of the Peralta camp did nothing to diminish the excitement of being on a mission together. Each knew what they had to do but could not help thinking of the other.

Manuel Peralta and Capitán Garces had their own thoughts to keep them awake that night. To each of them, the vision of U Day Ah in all her soft, feminine finery was enough to render them sleepless for most of the night. Even though neither of the two men held any real hope for a relationship with her, they could not help but dream. They had not been able to conceal their admiration of her from anyone—not from U Day Ah, and certainly not from O hi Cama. Don Miguel saw it. He was not happy about it.

———

Breakfast was accomplished without delay. Don Miguel wanted his guests to see that the Peralta expedition was operating as he had told Nanni Chaddi it would. Don Miguel escorted the Yavapai on their grand tour of the camp. In so doing, he made certain that neither Manuel nor el capitán was anywhere close to them. The one thing that Don Miguel wanted them to see and remember was the last item on his guided tour. He made sure that they witnessed the guards on patrol around the hill below the ruins of the Ancient Ones and the Rock in the Shape of a Man's Head. Nanni Chaddi must be thoroughly convinced that Don Miguel was keeping his word not to desecrate these sacred areas.

U Day Ah had never been even close to these sacred shrines. She looked at them for a long time, trying to understand the significance of them. She was awed by them. The Rock in the Shape of a Man's Head dominated her vision. It was so big! It was as tall as three wagons stacked end to end.

But when she looked at O hi Cama, his face was as a mask to her. She could not believe that he was showing no emotion at all. Then she realized that Don Miguel was looking directly at O hi Cama, trying to read the same thoughts that she was. O hi Cama would never allow his face to show his thoughts to Don Miguel. It was only when Don Miguel turned to go back toward the main area of camp that she saw O hi Cama's body shudder for just an instant. When he turned to follow Don Miguel, she saw the hatred come to his eyes.

That look told U Day Ah all she needed to know about how sacred this place was to the Yavapai and the extent to which the Yavapai (and even the Apache) would go to cleanse it of these intruders.

Back in the Peralta camp, the guests prepared to return to the Yavapai camp on the Rio Verde. It would be a long ride through harsh desert terrain. The sun was beating hot on the pair as they made their farewells.

The long ride back was filled with mostly silence between the two Yavapai. U Day Ah was allowing her thoughts to run the full gamut of sights, emotions, and concerns of what she had seen, and what had transpired. The effect the camp and the Peraltas had on O hi Cama was of utmost interest to her. What he would relate to Nanni Chaddi was important, of course. But what he thought about her and her relationship with Manuel Peralta and Capitán Garces was uppermost in her mind. His face did not tell her anything.

The look he had shown as they left the Rock in the Shape of a Man's Head had told her one sure thing: nothing would stop the Yavapai from eventually attacking the Peralta expedition.

Because she had lived among the non-Yavapai for so long and had travelled with the Peralta expedition, U Day Ah would be asked to explain what had been seen at the Peralta camp, and to translate their possible intentions. She could not help but feel torn between two cultures. She was Yavapai. Yet she had had a friendly relationship with these intruders into the land of the Yavapai. She had seen much violence and cruelty in her young life. She was afraid that she was to see more of it. She began to wonder if, as time progressed, she would remain U Day Ah or become Warrior Woman.

20

Don Miguel Peralta, mounted, made his way from the main camp up the canyon trail to his stone cabin. His mind rambled over the events of the past few weeks. The visit to the Yavapai camp on the Rio Verde, the invitational visit by U Day Ah and O hi Cama, and the eventual consequences of both of these ran continuously through his mind. Don Peralta had envisioned immediate war with the Apache and Yavapai after returning to the Sombrero Mines. Yet here they all were, at least on the surface, behaving as friendly neighbors. Unbelievable!

And these visits had continued for many weeks.

However, Don Miguel Peralta was no fool. He had grave doubts that this would continue. But he could not help but feel that he could make it last until he could exit for Mexico. Even if Nanni Chaddi was playing for time, so was he. Evidently, each felt that the more time each could buy was selfishly for the better. This, the don felt, played right into his plan. Overall, Don Peralta felt relieved and convinced that, at least for a while, a war would not happen.

Augmenting his feeling of security was the fact that the heat of summer had begun. Temperatures well in excess of one hundred degrees Fahrenheit did not accommodate warfare in the desert. Don Miguel Peralta began to breathe a little easier.

Don Peralta was shaken from his thoughts by a miner riding up the canyon to the cabin. Reining his mount to a halt, the miner announced, "Two riders, not Indians, are approaching the camp from downstream Camp Creek."

Don Peralta turned and joined the miner riding down the canyon to the main camp. When he arrived, he heard yelling and gunshots. It turned out that the guns were being fired into the air in celebration. Looking downstream, in the direction of the gunshots, he saw Manuel Peralta riding around and around the two riders in the wash. As they entered the camp, he recognized the reason for Manuel's excitement: Ramón!

The joyous laughter and embraces lasted for many minutes. Brother and brother, father and son, were reunited. As the celebration wound down, Don Peralta asked, more in exclamation than questioning, "What are you doing here!"

For a moment, silence hung thick in the hot summer air.

"Father, I bring news," replied the youngest son of the don. "Let us move into the shade of the tent."

"What news? Is my family well?" concernedly asked Don Peralta.

"Yes, Father. Pedro and his family are doing very well, and they all send you and Manuel their love," replied Ramón.

"Well, then . . . ?" said Don Miguel.

"Is there no cool water or anything even a might stronger in your tent?" asked Ramón.

The water was provided. "You are too young to drink anything stronger," said Manuel, laughing.

"Speak, boy!" commanded Don Miguel.

"Father, Don Enrique Vasquez came to our rancheria. But just before he arrived, a courier rode in with urgent news. He delivered a dispatch from our managers in California," answered Ramón. "Don Enrique advised us to get this information to you."

Don Miguel and Manuel both came to attention at this comment. Ramón continued. "The American courts in northern California are demanding original copies of the land grants giving the Peralta family title to the lands we are working there."

"Copies of such documents have been in the courts' possession for decades," said Don Peralta.

"Yes, Father. But they do not recognize the people we designate to manage those properties. They insist that the primary owner appear to certify the documents with originals," explained Ramón Peralta.

"What . . . this must happen now?" interjected Manuel.

"Yes," said Ramón. "And much time has elapsed since they issued the order."

"This means that I must go to California," said the don.

"How can you go now?" said Manuel. "You are needed here."

"I do not know," said the don. "I must have some time to think about it. Get settled, Ramón. See to it that Ramón's Yaqui guide, Emiliano, is well cared for, Manuel. I will eat my supper in my cabin tonight. I will see you all in the morning."

"There is one more thing, Father," said Ramón. "I do not know how this will affect this expedition."

"There is more?" asked Don Miguel. "Then speak up, Son."

Ramón took a deep breath and said, "El Presidente Santa Anna is no longer presidente of Mexico. He has been forced into exile. The government is in various forms of chaos. No one knows now what will happen."

"Santa Anna was a major source of funding for our expedition. He could be a great friend, but he could also be a terrible enemy," said Don Miguel Peralta. "There is much now to consider."

With that, Don Miguel Peralta excused himself and rode alone up to the stone cabin, away from the bustle of the camp. There, he would remain all night pondering the news brought by his youngest son over a long and very dangerous trail.

Sleep did not come easily for Don Miguel Peralta that night. There was so much for him to consider:

His youngest son, Ramón, had made a very difficult trek, with his Yaqui guide, through the desert heat and very possible Apache attack.

His good friend Don Enrique Vasquez, alcalde of Cananea, felt that the events happening in California were important enough to advise Pedro and Ramón Peralta that such a trek was necessary.

The Peralta land in California was so extremely important to the prosperity of the Peralta family that the legal problems must be addressed immediately.

El Presidente Santa Anna was now no longer a factor in this expedition. And yet:

The Sombrero Mines were producing more gold, more than he had imagined.

The danger of attack by the Yavapai was still a very dangerous possibility. That danger could be mitigated by the intervention of U Day Ah.

Could Manuel, with the help of Capitán Garces, be able to finish the Sombrero mining operation successfully?

Could Manuel and Capitán Garces safely return the expedition to Mexico?

— · —

By morning, Don Miguel Peralta had made his decision.

Breakfast found Manuel Peralta, Ramón Peralta, Capitán Garces, Lieutenant DaVia, and the Yaqui guide, Emiliano, awaiting Don Miguel. They did not have long to wait. Don Miguel Peralta arrived with determination showing in his stride. Coffee was served immediately to the don, and all awaited his decision.

"Gentlemen, I am glad to find you all here," said the don. "Ramón and Emiliano, today you must rest yourselves. You have had a tough journey. But tomorrow we leave for California. We must not delay more than is necessary to rest and supply ourselves."

"But Father . . ." began Manuel.

"Do not interrupt, Manuel," said the don. "I cannot jeopardize our important holdings in California. I must remit control of the Sombrero Mines to you, Manuel."

After a moment's hesitation, "I will not fail you," promised Manuel.

"Hear my orders," commanded Don Miguel Peralta. "Manuel, you will be in complete command of this expedition. Capitán Garces, I know I can count on you to support him just as if I were here in person. Until now, you and your cavalry were under the orders of El Presidente Santa Anna. He is in exile. The government is in disarray. No one probably knows what your military status is at the moment. You and your men are desperately needed here with this expedition. Therefore, I choose to make you all shareholders in the profits of our mining venture. Do you understand and agree?"

"Yes," came the reply from the officers, including Lieutenant DaVia.

The don continued. "The Yavapai must continue to be treated with respect. The girl, U Day Ah, must be treated with friendliness and nothing else. Do you both understand and agree?"

"Yes," came the reply from both men.

"Hear me now," continued Don Miguel. "We are making great prog-ress in the volume of gold stored in our warehouse at the cabin. We must not be overly greedy. Let me make this clear: under no circumstances are you to delay returning home to Mexico beyond the first cool weather of autumn. When you depart, do so without any delay. Leave the re-maining wagons behind. Speed will be most important until you pass the mountain called Superstition. This is very important. The Yavapai will not follow past that point. However, the Apache could attack from anywhere. Do you understand?

"Gentlemen," said the don, "do I have anything to worry about con-cerning the command and implementation of these orders?"

"No, sir," was the joint reply.

"Manuel, you will assume command immediately. Ramón and Emil-iano, we leave at dawn for California. We must head southwest to the Rio Gila on to Yuma to cross the Rio Colorado. It will be hot. We must carry more water than we would expect to use, but I would rather do that than run out of it. Manuel, see to it that we have all that we will need, not just for us, but for the horses, too. Now, just as Ramón and Emiliano, I am going to get some rest."

Don Miguel Peralta, his youngest son Ramón, and the Yaqui Emil-iano were moving southwest before morning light.

Until that morning, Manuel Peralta had merely to follow his father's orders and occasionally show some initiative. It had been quite an ad-venture so far. It was time to show his mettle. The son was in command. Command is a whole different world than that of a subordinate. The responsibility for the expedition rested on Manuel Peralta. Whether he would ever live to become a "don," or even if he were just going to live, was up to him alone . . . and he knew it. The weight of this knowledge came heavily to rest upon Manuel Peralta.

Yet even as the shadowy figure of his father, Don Miguel Peralta, fad-ed into the half-light of dawn, Manuel Peralta turned away and, standing tall and straight, took command.

21

Manuel Peralta, in complete command of the Peralta mining expedition, began to realize just how hard his father, Don Miguel, had had to work to keep this operation moving forward. He was early to rise in the morning and late to bed down at night. He began to rely heavily on Capitán Garces more and more as the days passed. But the work continued, and the gold stores grew and grew.

But the summer was so very, very hot. The men in the mines could not work the hours that they had worked earlier in the season. It was not cool in the shafts of the mines. It was much hotter than the outside temperature. Manuel arranged for the men to work in hour-long relays. Men would have died if it were not for this. The Yavapai scouts saw all this and reported it directly to O hi Cama. Nanni Chaddi was then given all information.

Nanni Chaddi remembered that, when he was young, no such relays were provided to the Yavapai working in those holes. He hated the memory of those days, but he began to realize that the summer's heat was bearing down on those men. They were probably becoming tired of this work. Nerves were probably always at the fraying point. Life was beginning to be only just bearable for those miners. In addition to taking some satisfaction from their pain, he realized that they would be likely to violate the agreement between Don Miguel and himself soon. He expected the sacred areas to remain so, because it could be done with the guard patrols. But soon someone would discover another place where the yellow stones could be dug. That would violate the agreement: *"no more holes."*

The visits to the Peralta camp were accomplished less often. Nothing was being gained by them except to keep the smiles coming. The Yavapai scouts were in a better position to note any new mining activities.

On one such visit, U Day Ah was speaking with Manuel Peralta and el capitán in the shade of a ramada near their tent. Due to the strict order of Don Miguel prior to his departure, neither of the caballeros had been showing their infatuation for U Day Ah. She noticed it and accepted it. O hi Cama noticed it but did not trust it. Yet he saw nothing to provoke his anger. As always, he was a silent sentinel watching over U Day Ah.

The two caballeros were jolted out of the laziness of the afternoon by the voice of O hi Cama, who rose to his feet and bluntly asked, "Where is your chieftain?" Manuel had hoped that the absence of Don Miguel would not be noticed. This was foolish, of course, yet it took two visits for the Yavapai to miss the don.

Manuel also rose, but slowly so as not to arouse any particular reaction. Capitán Garces, who had been enjoying the beauty of U Day Ah, was taken aback somewhat by the sudden question. He recovered quickly and smiled at U Day Ah. Manuel told O hi Cama, "My father, Don Miguel, was summoned to meet some men farther west to solve a problem concerning cattle. He did not wish to go, but he felt it important to do so." He then added, "He will return as soon as his business is completed."

O hi Cama slowly sat down again and continued his uninterested stare. Manuel was not sure whether he believed his story. He was truthful about his father's departure, but he hoped the lie about his eventual return was not noticed. Evidently, U Day Ah wished to show a little more interest and asked, "Who came to notify your father, Manuel?"

Manuel replied, to avoid any seeming deception, "My younger brother, Ramón, made the trek all the way from our home in southern Sonora. He brought news that a problem of great importance for our family must be addressed. The fact that he came so far to inform Don Miguel shows how important he thought it was."

"More important than the mission of this expedition?" asked U Day Ah.

Manuel saw where this line of questioning was headed and said, "My father, Don Miguel, is pleased with how well our work here has been going. However, he is even more pleased that the Yavapai have chosen to allow him to finish this work. He is very grateful, and, because of the friendship of the Yavapai, he feels he can attend to this other matter."

U Day Ah related this to O hi Cama. The warrior actually made an attempt to smile upon hearing this. Manuel and el capitán were not sure what he meant by that smile. However, Lieutenant Diego DaVia, just then passing by the ramada, thought he knew. But he kept walking and said nothing.

Later, the visit ended with the usual smiles and waves, and the Yavapai left on what had become, due to frequent use, an actual trail between the two camps.

Warrior Woman rode slowly beside O hi Cama. Both were deep in thought over what had just transpired in the Peralta camp. Warrior Woman could not help thinking about the reaction of el capitán to O hi Cama's question as to the whereabouts of Don Miguel. He covered it well, but she sensed the underlying tension. She could understand the fact that the Yavapai were not notified by Don Miguel that he was leaving. However, the reaction on the part of el capitán disturbed her.

She watched the face of O hi Cama as they rode. He rode facing straight ahead, showing no emotion whatsoever. But his eyes told her all she wanted to know. He, too, caught the tension regarding the departure of Don Miguel. He, too, understood that there was no reason for Don Miguel to notify Nanni Chaddi of his departure. O hi Cama saw beyond that. He saw no reason but an attempt at deception by the Peraltas in not speaking of it the day before when the Yavapai arrived at their camp. Why did it require a direct question by himself to be told of it? He believed that the rules of this game had just changed.

It was late when they entered the Rio Verde camp. Nanni Chaddi was standing alone by the fire awaiting them. O hi Cama motioned him to the wikiup. Without a word, the three entered the wikiup and sat down. Nanni Chaddi spoke. "O hi Cama, your look tells me something is new at the Peralta camp. What is it?"

"Their chief, Don Miguel Peralta, has left the expedition. His son, Manuel, said that he had been summoned far away to attend to some problem for the family," began O hi Cama.

"When did this happen?" asked Nanni Chaddi.

"It has been two, maybe three weeks past," answered O hi Cama.

"How is it that we are only now hearing of this?" asked Nanni Chaddi.

"It has been nearly ten days since our last visit to their camp, my chief. I took no notice that Don Miguel was gone then because some visits we do not see him," answered O hi Cama.

Warrior Woman sought to explain further. "On this visit, O hi Cama noticed that he was not to be seen, and so asked the son directly about his missing father."

O hi Cama spoke again. "The son, Manuel Peralta, answered as if nothing was wrong, but el capitán's eyes showed alarm. He recovered and went back to looking at Warrior Woman."

Nanni Chaddi then turned to Warrior Woman and asked, "What do you think about this, Warrior Woman?"

"I think that they are trying to finish their mission without their chieftain to lead them. I think that they are insecure about their situation. They are very nervous," said Warrior Woman.

"I think the weakness that we have been awaiting has shown itself," said Nanni Chaddi.

"The son, Manuel Peralta, is in command of the expedition now. He may be new to command, but I did not see any violation of the agreement made with his father," offered Warrior Woman.

Nanni Chaddi thought for a moment in silence, then said, "O hi Cama, are you thinking, as I am, that the time is near to drive these men from our midst?"

"But they have not violated the terms of the agreement!" said Warrior Woman, without realizing for a brief moment that she was thinking like "U Day Ah" in this.

Nanni Chaddi chose not to notice this. O hi Cama then said, "Warrior Woman, you are right. But now, with their chieftain gone, they *will* violate it. We will watch and see."

"There will now be no more visits to their camp. We will continue our patrols from a distance. At the first sign of treachery, I will send runners to our friends, the Apache, requesting a counsel," said Nanni Chaddi.

O hi Cama added his part in this plan. "I will watch them from areas that we have not before. I have seen men going back and forth up the canyon where the Peraltas have made the stone cabin. I will circle around and observe from the south what is happening in that canyon."

"Yes, O hi Cama, I am familiar with it. The ridge on the south side of that canyon is very high and irregular. You will not be seen, but you will be able to see all that occurs from there," agreed Nanni Chaddi.

"I will wait three days before I go there," said O hi Cama. "They may be extra vigilant for a day or so. But after that, they may show a different face."

With that, O hi Cama left the wikiup of Nanni Chaddi. The Yavapai chief motioned to Warrior Woman to remain. "Warrior Woman, you showed a moment of concern over whether these men had violated the agreement between Don Miguel and the Yavapai. Do you have feeling for these men?" asked Nanni Chaddi.

"As you have said, Nanni Chaddi, I have become Warrior Woman. But I am also U Day Ah! I hated the Mexican/Apache village and the people where I was a captive. I was treated as less than an animal by them. The Mexican soldiers who took me from the village were less than human," said Warrior Woman.

"I understand all that happened to you, Warrior Woman," sadly stated Nanni Chaddi.

"Yet the men of the Peraltas were kind to me. They gave me back my life. I am once again a Yavapai woman because of them. I know the young men of their camp have looked at me. But they have not forced themselves upon me. I find it hard to hate them," said Warrior Woman with tears in her eyes.

"Warrior Woman, you are very wise. I agree with you in all that you have said to me. There are good and bad in all peoples. There are good and bad Yavapai. But we, as Yavapai, have seen what these men can do. Many Yavapai and many Mexicans were killed when these men were here last. I will make you this promise, Warrior Woman," advanced Nanni Chaddi. "If these men honor their promise to not dig any more holes in Earth Mother, I will give them time to make their way from here in safety. But if they violate the promises of Don Miguel Peralta to me and the Yavapai people, I will show them no mercy. We will then see if these new Mexicans can fight!"

Warrior Woman saw that, what Nanni Chaddi had said it would be, was the way it must be. Slowly she rose to her feet and said quietly, "Nanni Chaddi, you are chief of all the Yavapai. You are the keeper of our people. I see the wisdom in what you say. U Day Ah will always remain within me, but Warrior Woman will faithfully serve the Yavapai."

With that, dreading what might come, she left for her wikiup, alone.

22

O hi Cama left Nanni Chaddi's wikiup with the intention of getting some sleep in his own. By the time he stood outside the wikiup, he had made up his mind to just keep on going. He caught another horse, swung up on his back, and rode swiftly out of the Rio Verde Camp. His emotions were running very high. O hi Cama, the warrior, wanted to attack these Mexican intruders immediately. They had no right to be here!

Yet he was learning much from Nanni Chaddi. One of these things was restraint. He was learning how hard it was to stop, think about what might happen before it does, and then do what your logic says is best. He was finding it so difficult. Nanni Chaddi had seen something in him and because of it had given him much more responsibility among the warriors of the Yavapai. O hi Cama needed some time to put his thoughts and emotions in order.

The problem, he knew, was not the Mexicans. Some day he would fight them or not fight them. However, there was Warrior Woman, U Day Ah. She had his mind whirling. He honored and respected Warrior Woman. Unfortunately, he knew he was completely in love with U Day Ah . . . same woman yet different. O hi Cama thought she desired to be his woman. Then he saw how the two Mexican caballeros looked at her. Those men seemed to think that she should be with them.

He had said he would spy on the Peralta camp from the south in three days. He would spend all of those three days alone in the remote desert. Right now, he needed to be alone. A three-hour ride, in the dark, upstream on the Rio Verde, placed him in a remote area of river, woods, and rock formations. It contained no people. Here he planned to stay for nearly three days.

Warrior Woman spent the entire night wide-eyed yet teary-eyed. She could not remove the thought of O hi Cama losing interest in her. She had seen the look. She had seen jealousy before. She knew that he felt hurt that she might have some interest in those Mexican caballeros. She had been O hi Cama's woman from the moment she saw him standing in the Rio Verde camp. How would she ever be able to erase the thoughts that he must be thinking? She did not know.

O hi Cama could hardly know that her only interest in those men was that of friendliness. They had been kind to her. She was aware of their interest in her but only found it flattering. After all, she was a lovely young woman, and she knew it. So what?

Now the Yavapai may be about to attack these Mexicans. Warrior Woman saw the reasons for such action; however, U Day Ah did not wish harm to come to them. They had given her new life. She did not wish them to lose theirs. Clearly, she did not know what to think, much less what to do.

Next morning, red-eyed and somewhat disheveled, she moved around the camp as if in a trance. The other women noticed but said nothing. Some had heard her sobbing during the night. Nanni Chaddi left the fire and walked to her. The look in his eyes told her something had happened. He wasted no time. "O hi Cama rode out of camp during the night. His tracks led to the north, up the river."

"He said nothing?" asked Warrior Woman.

"No. But he had said he would seek out information from the Peralta camp in three days. This I know he will do," said Nanni Chaddi.

"I cannot wait three days or more to see him," said Warrior Woman. "I must make the bad thoughts he has of me fly away from him."

"You must make sure these thoughts have no meaning even to you," said Nanni Chaddi. "I am much older than you. You have no father, so I will speak to you as such. You must go, yourself, to clear any confusion from your own mind. If you were a male warrior, I would send you to the steam house to be cleansed and starved into having a 'vision.' I believe you must go away alone, as has O hi Cama, to make your spirit pure. I have spoken."

Warrior Woman slowly sank to her knees by the fire. Her head sank to her chest. When she arose, she walked straight to her pinto pony. Without looking back, she rode out of camp northward along the river.

Nanni Chaddi had made his way back to his wikiup and barely took notice of Warrior Woman's departure. However, in order to head northward from the Rio Verde camp, she had to ride directly past his wikiup. Later, when asked, the women of the camp told him she had ridden slowly upstream northward. That way when she made a sharp left, heading southwest, no one was aware of it.

Warrior Woman was not thinking about what she would actually do by riding southwest toward the Peralta camp. She was beset by many thoughts and emotions that were strange to her. The hatred and fear that had consumed her entire being for the past few years, important years to a girl growing into womanhood, were being replaced by the softer feelings brought on by that very womanhood.

She knew that she had found love in the form of a fine young Yavapai warrior, O hi Cama. If possible, she would not do anything to lose his love for her, but her time with the Peraltas had shown her that not all Mexicans were her enemies. She just could not reconcile her mind to believe that they should all be killed. She was not in love with either of the young caballeros who had shown so much interest in her. But she had learned to care for them, as well as Sergeant Mendoza and others who had been so kind to her. There must be a way to avoid the pain and suffering of a fight for both the Mexicans and the Yavapai. There just must be!

Oblivious to anything else, onward she rode.

23

Sebriano, one of the many miners enlisted in the Peralta expedition, had made this trip often, way too often as far as he was concerned. Carrying gold to the main camp and returning with supplies, in this unbearable desert heat, had become just one big pain to him. He wanted to go home. His home was nothing special itself, but it held a special attraction just for him. He had a girlfriend there. She was young and lovely, and he missed her. He had no permanent plans for her. He did not love her enough to marry her. But she made the nights better. Sebriano enjoyed sleeping close to her. He had been without his woman, any woman, way too long to suit him.

It was midday and hot. He had made his way around the outcropping of low hills northeast of the main Peralta camp. Shade was on his mind at the moment. He saw the palo verde tree ahead and made for it. Then, something caught his eye. Something had moved on the far side of the palo verde tree. Sebriano stopped dead in his tracks in fear. The Yavapai had been everywhere lately. Not wishing to meet up with them, he guided his mule into the creosote thicket nearby, but off the trail. There he waited in silence.

After just a few moments, he saw a movement again. This time he recognized who it was. The slim form of U Day Ah moved from her pinto pony farther into the shade of the palo verde. She took water from her pouch and took a drink. She was close to the Peralta camp but was undecided as to whether she dared to enter alone. She was not sure even why she had made this ride to their camp. Presently, she came to the realization that she merely wanted to be sure she and the Yavapai were right in hating these people. After all, she felt that she had friends among the Mexicans.

She stood up to go to her pony and proceed to the Peralta camp. As she did so, strong arms encircled her and dragged her to the ground. Sebriano had seen U Day Ah, and remembering how beautiful she had looked in their camps as she travelled with them, he could not resist the temptation she offered out here in the desert . . . alone!

U Day Ah managed just one terrified scream before a rough hand was clamped over her mouth. She fought back in silence, trying to force this unknown attacker off her. Scratching and biting, she managed to push him far enough away from her to recognize his face. She had seen this man before in the Peralta expedition. She remembered the face as one of many who had watched her with eyes that spoke forcefully of what would happen if she strayed from the protection of the Peraltas. U Day Ah had been rescued from low-life creatures just such as this. Now again, alone in the desert, she was in the grasp of one of these animals.

She felt herself being thrown back on the ground. She rolled violently to avoid being pinned there under this man. Having been somewhat thwarted by her move, Sebriano angrily growled something at her and rose up to strike her with his fist. U Day Ah never felt that fist, but instead, she felt the hard impact of a blow delivered to Sebriano. He rolled off her and, seizing his long hunting knife, leaped to meet this intruder who had struck him so violently. A flash of steel, the swishing sound as it slashed forward, and a loud curse from Sebriano split the air as the blade slashed his arm. Sebriano lunged forward to throw his knife at his attacker. The long blade of the saber shot through his chest, once and then twice, as he looked upon the face of the man who had just killed him. U Day Ah recognized him . . . Lieutenant Diego DaVia.

U Day Ah fought the urge to faint as Lieutenant DaVia calmly raised her to a sitting position. His words reassured her that she was all right and that he meant her no harm. Once she had gathered herself and was able to assess the situation, she became aware that Lieutenant DaVia had moved away from her and was visibly shaking as if chilled. Evidently, killing a man in battle was one thing. Having to exterminate an animal like Sebriano was another.

Once in control of himself, Lieutenant DaVia asked, "Are you able to travel? Are you hurt other than just frightened by that animal?"

U Day Ah answered as best she could, "Yes, I can travel."

Then Lieutenant DaVia's calm voice became raspy with some anger shown in it. "What the hell were you doing here? Were you going to the Peralta camp?"

She started to answer *yes* but stopped upon seeing the look on his face.

"Understand me, woman," he said. "You know you are a beautiful young woman. You know that there are no other women, beautiful or otherwise, in that camp. Even if you were not Yavapai, you would be in trouble there. You are not stupid. Why would you go there? Alone!"

U Day Ah wanted to say that she wished to see her friends, but she could not speak those words. She had seen this man in the Peralta camp while she was with them and had judged Lieutenant DaVia to be a dangerous man. He had just been kind to her. He had rescued her from being raped by that animal Sebriano. But he was a dangerous man. After all, she had just seen him run his saber through the chest of one of his own men, twice. When she spoke, all that she could say was, "I must leave here!"

Lieutenant DaVia answered, "You certainly must leave here." He then added, "I do not know why you were here in the first place. I know not what you will tell your people but hear this: all we want to do is get out of here. We mean your people no harm in spite of what this animal tried to do to you."

U Day Ah then said, "I wish you no harm."

Lieutenant DaVia said, "I hope not. I believe I know what is in the heart of your chief, Nanni Chaddi, and in the heart of that fierce warrior O hi Cama. I just hope that we can pull out of here before they do something stupid."

U Day Ah had, with the lieutenant's assistance, mounted her pinto pony.

U Day Ah started to say something, but Lieutenant DaVia interrupted. "If your people attack, there will be a great fight. Many will die— your warriors, my soldiers. There is no point to that. It is not necessary.

But if the Yavapai want to be destroyed, they will find that we are not weak. They cannot win!"

"We are not alone! What will happen . . . will happen!" angrily shouted Warrior Woman.

With that, Lieutenant DaVia slapped her pony on the rump and sent U Day Ah on her way back to her people.

24

Lieutenant DaVia stood there for a few moments, watching U Day Ah disappear into the desert hills. His thoughts raced from one to another as she raced away. He had just saved this beautiful young girl from being raped again, by a Mexican. He had just killed, by the saber at his side, a fellow Mexican of the Peralta expedition. He had told U Day Ah, in so many words, that she was not welcome in the Peralta camp alone and that she might be harmed. As if that were not enough, he had challenged the Yavapai to a fight if they wanted it. He told them that they could not win against the Peralta expedition.

"*Dios mio!* Why did I not just start shooting!" he exclaimed to himself.

Lieutenant DaVia took the time to bury Sebriano just off the trail near the palo verde tree. The last thing he wanted to do was to arrive in camp with a dead body. Either a war would start, or desertions would begin. He would just keep his mouth shut for a while. If pressured by Manuel Peralta or el capitán, he would tell them what happened but, hopefully, not now.

It was late afternoon when Lieutenant DaVia rode into camp. He had already had quite a day but would report to el capitán first, anyway. When asked, a miner told him that el capitán was up at the stone cabin of Don Miguel's. He turned his horse up the canyon toward the cabin. A short distance along the canyon, he saw Manuel and el capitán riding toward him. He stopped to wait for them. As they approached him, Lieutenant DaVia let his tired eyes wander along the canyon wall. What he saw made him react so violently that his horse reared and pawed the air. Manuel Peralta and Capitán Garces arrived to: "What the hell! Have you both lost your minds? Are you trying to get us all killed?" screamed Lieutenant DaVia. "Why have you started another mine shaft in this canyon?"

"Relax, Lieutenant. Control yourself," ordered el capitán.

"Lieutenant DaVia, we had a sudden storm here two nights ago. The rain washed open a vein of gold-bearing quartz. I ordered it excavated, and it has produced much gold already," said Manuel Peralta.

Lieutenant DaVia, barely managing to speak in his low, level tone, asked, "Do you not remember the promise Don Miguel made to that Yavapai chief? You know, the one that said we would not open any more holes in their Earth Mother?"

"Of course, I do. But this is secluded along the wall of this canyon. No one will see it. We will take the gold now. And the Yavapai will see it after we are gone," Manuel Peralta replied, laughing.

"Do you not understand, Manuel? Your father understood," said Lieutenant DaVia.

"You forget your place, Lieutenant! I understand that I, Manuel Peralta, am in charge now . . . not my father," asserted Manuel. "My father, Don Miguel Peralta, transferred full command to me, Manuel Peralta. Is this not the Peralta expedition? And are these not the Peralta mines? I will do as I see fit to do. Do you understand, Lieutenant DaVia?"

"Yes, I understand!" snapped Lieutenant DaVia. Having spoken that, the lieutenant and el capitán rode back down to the main camp and their tents.

After supper, Capitán Garces was not surprised to see Lieutenant DaVia approach his tent.

"What can I do for you, Lieutenant?" asked the capitán, expecting some dissension on the part of Lieutenant DaVia.

"Capitán, we are charged to provide protection for the Peraltas, of which there is now only one, and the Peralta miners. All this in order to make sure that as much gold is brought back to Mexico as possible. Do I understand these orders correctly?" asked Lieutenant DaVia.

"You do," answered el capitán.

"How much gold do you believe we can return to Mexico, if we have to fight a running battle during the better part of the trip?" calmly asked the lieutenant.

El capitán really did not want this conversation to deteriorate into a game of rank, a "who takes orders from whom" sort of thing. He therefore simply stated, "Diego, something else is on your mind. Tell me."

"Capitán, you and I need to think this through. Manuel Peralta just wants to bring back more gold than his father thinks he can. But he has lost sight of the fact that if he does not get back at all, who will care about the gold?" said Lieutenant DaVia.

"We are Mexican cavalry, Lieutenant," said el capitán. "Let us not forget that, even out here, we are a military organization with orders to provide safety to this expedition."

"I agree, Capitán. But we started out here as cavalry under the orders of El Presidente Santa Anna. With Santa Anna in exile, we don't really know whom we serve. I don't even know if legally we are still an authorized military unit. With that in mind, it does not matter anyway if we don't get back alive, does it?" stated Lieutenant DaVia.

"Your point is well taken, Lieutenant. Proceed," said el capitán.

"I had hoped not to disclose this until a later time, but there may not be a much later time now. I have brought the miner Sebriano's gold and mule to camp. Today, I had to kill Sebriano with my saber, Capitán," said Lieutenant DaVia. "No, let me go on," he said as el capitán reacted by starting to stand. "Sebriano was trying his very best to rape the Yavapai girl, U Day Ah, a short way from here along the trail."

El capitán was momentarily speechless.

Lieutenant DaVia continued, "He was holding her down and fighting to remove her clothes when I killed him. U Day Ah recovered, but when I asked, she could not or would not tell me what she was doing so close to our main camp. The look in her eyes told me that Sebriano had probably removed any good feeling for any of us by his actions."

El capitán could only ask, "What do you think she will do now?"

"I cannot imagine," said Lieutenant DaVia. "However, I tried to assure her that we just wanted to leave this place as soon as we can. Her eyes were telling me plenty. I told her that we do not want to fight her people, that many would die on both sides. I told her that if her people attack, we will fight. We are not weak. We will not be driven out."

"Evidently, we will not be seeing U Day Ah anymore here at this camp," said el capitán.

"I think the friendly visits are over, Capitán. If we see her anymore, it will be only as an interpreter for her people," said the lieutenant.

"So, Lieutenant, your message is this: we need to get the hell out of here! Am I correct, Lieutenant?" asked el capitán.

"Yes, sir!" was Lieutenant DaVia's enthusiastic reply.

Manuel Peralta had been extremely pleased about being named by his father, Don Miguel, to take command of the Peralta expedition. He was convinced that his father had named him because he was most worthy of the position. Although he was saddened by Don Miguel's departure, he was inwardly elated by his elevation in status. Manuel Peralta was determined to use his command position to bring back to Sonora the most gold possible. He would allow nothing to prevent his achieving that goal.

Shortly after Don Miguel departed with Ramón Peralta and Emiliano for California, Manuel Peralta began asserting his authority. He called a meeting of the military officers and non-commissioned officers, along with the squad leaders of the large contingent of miners. Rules of conduct, work schedules and labor load, reporting of incidents, and transporting of ore and processed gold to the warehouse for accounting were revisited. All present were given their assignments. Not everyone was overjoyed at the new assignments but found themselves with no alternative propositions.

The military, namely El Capitán Garces and Lieutenant DaVia, were not at all pleased by this new arrangement. They had been working *with* Don Miguel. The relationship was one of working together toward a common goal. Neither el capitán nor Lieutenant DaVia relished working *for* Manuel Peralta.

Manuel Peralta, although having served in the Mexican army toward the end of the war with the United States, had held the rank of second lieutenant, primarily because he joined as the son of the prominent Don Miguel Peralta. He fought bravely and well and was decorated for his bravery. Yet Manuel did not achieve the level of expertise in that short time to be promoted. He lacked experience in command. El capitán followed Manuel's orders more in deference to Don Miguel's instruction than because Manuel had a commanding presence. Therefore, Manuel's new commanding stature began to wear a bit thin on el capitán and Lieutenant DaVia.

The relationship between Manuel and el capitán had deteriorated to the point that, in light of the dire possibilities concerning the meeting of Lieutenant DaVia and U Day Ah, el capitán relished putting the matter right smack in Manuel Peralta's lap. Neither he, nor Lieutenant DaVia, saw any reason to delay. Together, they rode directly up the canyon to Manuel Peralta's stone cabin.

There was very little daylight left. Dusk was upon the two cavalry officers as they dismounted in front of the stone cabin of Manuel Peralta. Lieutenant DaVia knocked once loudly on the door in typical military fashion.

"I see you, gentlemen. Please come in," said Manuel Peralta. "Smoke if you wish. What can I do for you this evening?"

El capitán spoke in a low tone and politely. "There has been a development about which we both felt you should know."

"What is it?" asked Manuel.

"U Day Ah was very close to our camp this afternoon," began el capitán.

"So?" interrupted Manuel. "What was she doing here?"

"When I saw her, she was being raped," interjected Lieutenant DaVia.

"Whaaat!" exclaimed Manuel. "By whom? Is she all right? Is she here?"

"By Sebriano, a miner . . . sort of all right . . . no, she is not here," answered Lieutenant DaVia, somewhat sarcastically. At this point, el capitán just stepped back and allowed Lieutenant DaVia to have his say. "Sebriano is dead. I know because I ran him through twice with my handy little cavalry saber, and then I buried him. U Day Ah, having been almost raped, went back to her people. But before she left, we had a little talk. What little was said was doubled by the look on her face. I told her we wanted just to leave here at the earliest opportunity, without any trouble. Her look told me plenty. So, I told her that I knew what the Yavapai were thinking. I warned her that they had better not attack, because we are not weak. There would be much death on both sides."

Manuel Peralta sat down hard, stunned by his words. "What did she say to that?" he asked.

"She shouted, 'What will happen . . . will happen!'" answered Lieutenant DaVia. "Then I slapped her pinto on the butt and sent her on her way."

Manuel Peralta, still seated, asked, "What do you gentlemen feel we should do?"

A slight pause ensued until el capitán spoke. "I think Lieutenant DaVia has the right idea. We need to get the hell out of here as soon as possible!"

"What? Just because a Yavapai girl does not like us anymore?" questioned Manuel.

El capitán said to Lieutenant DaVia, "Tell Manuel what else you think about the Yavapai plan, Diego."

"The Yavapai have been recruiting other tribes to help them. She screamed at me that they were not alone. I'm guessing Apache," said Lieutenant DaVia.

"Go on," said el capitán.

"I believe they are doing the same thing we are . . . waiting for the right time. The Yavapai and this outfit are both waiting for cooler weather because no one wants to fight in this abominable damn heat. They don't have all their friends committed yet. We want all the gold we can carry, and we're also waiting for cooler weather for the long, hard trek to Sonora," said the lieutenant.

"So . . . what is new?" asked Manuel. "We've known all along, on our part anyway, that the cool weather would see us leave here."

"Manuel, listen to me! This problem with the girl has surely made up the Yavapai's mind. But they need something else to draw the other tribes into it. Defiling the Earth Mother, near their Ancient Ones, is sure to bring everybody. You know what I mean . . . the new mine!" argued Lieutenant DaVia.

"No one will see that new hole in the ground," said Manuel. "To hell with it! To hell with those damn Yavapai! They are still a small band of savages. They will never gather enough warriors to stop this expedition."

"We hope not, but as the military leader here, I say they could wound us severely enough to ruin this whole effort!" said el capitán Garces, his voice rising.

"What do you suggest, Capitán?" asked Manuel Peralta.

"Start packing. Begin by immediately pulling in the miners from the remote mines. Arm them and use them to guard this camp. Extra men can begin packing for the long walk home," said Capitán Garces.

"Remember," advised Lieutenant DaVia, "we will need to move fast when we move. Those damn wagons stay here. We take everything on mules and horseback."

"We will wait until we know more from the Yavapai," said Manuel Peralta, reasserting himself as the leader of this operation. "But . . . without any show, we will begin packing essential items tomorrow."

The two military officers said their goodnights and left without smiling. As they rode down the canyon, the two agreed to begin as if the war had already started.

25

O hi Cama, upon arriving at the spot he wished to camp, dismounted, watered his horse, and sat down to think. He had believed that the ride would help him put his thoughts in proper order. He was wrong. Nothing made any sense. His mind ricocheted from one thought to another like an arrow loosed in a rocky canyon. But it always returned to the thought of U Day Ah asleep, helpless, and beautiful by the Rio Verde where he found her.

He then realized that he had just ridden three hours away from her. He also realized that it would take him another three hours to return to her. Six hours! To accomplish nothing but what he had always known anyway. Then O hi Cama, warrior of the Yavapai, remembered that he had another mission to fulfill. He had said that in three days he would spy on the Peralta encampment from the southern ridge. He was still convinced that there was treachery going on in that camp. Why wait three days? There was no reason why he could not return the long way, by circling around to the southern ridge of the Peralta camp en route to the Yavapai camp on the Rio Verde.

Having refreshed and rested his horse, O hi Cama mounted and turned west toward an area north of the Peralta camp. The way was long and required much ridge climbing through all manner of vegetation. It has been said that if anything is native to this desert, it will poke you, scratch you, or bite you. How true! O hi Cama was more than willing to make camp earlier than planned. Yet he was still in an area well north of the Peralta camp. A good night's rest would prepare him for the next day's ride, over more ridges to the southern ridge overlooking the Peralta encampment. O hi Cama made certain that his horse was not severely scratched, and also properly fed and watered before bedding down. He chewed on deer jerky until satisfied. Although ready for sleep, it was a long time coming.

O hi Cama was up early the next morning. Once again, his camp boasted no fire to give away his location. He ate a cold breakfast. Then, resolute of mind, he swung up on the back of his horse and guided him slowly and cautiously southward, up and over the next few ridges toward the Peraltas. He had to gently lead his horse to make the climb to the top of the ridge northwest of the Peralta cabin. A very high ridge curled around the mine and cabin that Manuel Peralta used as his headquarters. The mesquite and ironwood partially hid them as they made their way up the treacherous slopes. Once at the summit, he could slowly work his way around to a point from which he could see the entire canyon from the south, especially whatever was being done on the opposite north wall of that canyon.

The Yavapai warrior secured his horse out of sight and made his way to the top of the ridge. It was midday and exceedingly hot. No activity was to be seen below. The miners were hiding from the noonday heat. Whatever labor was to be done would be done later. O hi Cama would also use this time to rest. A small drink of water, a few bites of jerky, and the warrior closed his eyes.

O hi Cama took full advantage of the opportunity to catch a little rest during the hot midday heat. He was exhausted. The ride over the many high desert ridges was extremely trying for man and horse. The movement of the sun, as the afternoon wore on, changed the pattern of shade that had comforted him during his nap. He slowly awakened with the heat of the late afternoon sun beating down on him. He became aware of activity in the canyon below.

Miners were applying the picks and shovels of their trade as the sun sank lower and extended the shade of the ridge to cover their efforts. O hi Cama now became aware of the new ugly slice in the canyon wall directly across the wash from his position. The canyon wall was made up of rust-colored rocks, much darker than other areas of the canyon. It made the exposed white quartz vein stand out vividly against that very dark background. The sun shone brightly on the white quartz and illuminated the gold streaks running through it. The excited chatter of the miners added immensely to the irritation of O hi Cama as he witnessed this flagrant violation of the agreement between Don Miguel Peralta and Nanni Chaddi.

He had seen enough.

O hi Cama waited until the shadows had grown longer, enabling him the opportunity to move unseen eastward along the south ridge of the canyon. He had worked his way about a quarter of a mile to a point just south and west of the hilltop that contained the ruins of the homes of the Ancient Ones, when he stopped abruptly. There, about two-thirds up the side of the hill, miners were digging in an area of exposed white quartz. Don Miguel Peralta had sworn to protect this sacred place!

Enraged, O hi Cama skirted around the hill and the main Peralta encampment east of it, rode down Blue Wash, and crossed the Camp Creek wash at Blue Mountain. There, feeling safe from view of the Peraltas, he rode hard toward the Yavapai camp on the Rio Verde.

26

U Day Ah arrived in the Yavapai Rio Verde camp late in the afternoon. She was still emotionally shaken by the afternoon's events. She was U Day Ah when she rode toward the Peralta camp; however, it was Warrior Woman who entered her wikiup that evening. Her hatred for the Mexicans was reignited by her attempted rape at the hands of the Mexican Sebriano. She was immensely grateful for her rescue by Lieutenant DaVia, but any good feeling she might have had for him was irrevocably tempered by his stern warning to her and her people should the Peraltas be attacked.

However clouded her thoughts were that night, they became crystal clear by morning. She wanted the Peraltas gone from her homeland. Their presence, after returning to the Yavapai, had caused her nothing but anguish. U Day Ah longed to begin a life with O hi Cama even though he had never mentioned it to her. Yet, as the young woman she was, she knew such was in his heart. She also knew that it would never be, as long as the specter of her relationship with the Peraltas remained in his mind.

U Day Ah spent the day alone in her wikiup. She wished to speak to no one about her encounter with Lieutenant DaVia. All she wanted was to be alone. O hi Cama was, she thought, up in the country of the north Rio Verde. Nanni Chaddi had evidently left the Rio Verde camp also. Good. So be it. She could settle down for the day as merely a Yavapai woman, unencumbered by all these other problems.

That feeling of peace lasted all day. Then, as the fires of supper began to die down, O hi Cama rode into camp . . . from the southwest. He dismounted running. His face held a stern aspect as he searched for Nan-ni Chaddi. When he saw U Day Ah, his look softened, and he started toward her. However, one of the Yavapai alerted him that Nanni Chaddi had left for one of the northern encampments. His instruction was that he would not return for a few days.

Hearing this, O hi Cama asked that another pony be selected for him. He wished to follow Nanni Chaddi, but his own pony was exhausted. O hi Cama walked to U Day Ah. His look was soft as he told her he would have to leave immediately. His attention to her was noted by all. It was also noted that she asked him to delay for a moment, because she wished to send some food with him for his journey.

The fresh pony and the food from U Day Ah were delivered at the same time. Once remounted, the hard, determined look returned to the face of O hi Cama, and he disappeared into the night. U Day Ah watched as he rode out of camp and into the darkness. She knew, from his look and the urgency of his departure, that something important had happened. She hoped that it had nothing to do with her attempted rape. It would be better, right now, if he knew nothing about it. Instead, she would cling to that moment of concern shown by each for the other.

O hi Cama was very pleased by the pony chosen for him by the young warrior at the camp. It was strong, swift, and tough. It had to be tough. Riding through the rocky, brush-filled trail by daylight was no stroll. But at night, by moonlight, it was a rough ordeal. O hi Cama, real-izing how difficult it was on the animal, paused at frequent intervals. He might have considered getting a little sleep, but the thought of what the Peraltas were doing re-infuriated him so much that sleep was impossible. Therefore . . . onward he rode.

⸻

Just before the time of the noon meal, O hi Cama rode into the northern Yavapai camp. Normally he would have given early warning to the camp that he was coming in, but this was his own band's camp. Ever since he was a young boy, playing at being a warrior, he liked to alarm the village. They had come to expect it of him. This day was no different. He put his heels into the horse's ribs, yelled, and charged into the camp.

To O hi Cama's surprise, a number of arrows filled the air, coming perilously close. He leaped to the ground and, still running, raised his arms, laughing. Thank goodness Nanni Chaddi also laughed. The warriors of the camp, guarding it, did not like the humor in O hi Cama's charge. O hi Cama saw why. Visitors were in the camp . . . Apache!

Some half-dozen Apache warriors had leaped to their feet, along with Nanni Chaddi and a dozen more Yavapai, at this playful intrusion. Nanni Chaddi's warm greeting to O hi Cama put the others involved at ease. Now, with everyone already standing, Nanni Chaddi chose this time to make introductions. O hi Cama was introduced, in turn, to representatives of the Tonto Apache, Mescalero Apache, and the Chiricahua Apache. Upon realizing who O hi Cama was, namely Nanni Chaddi's war subchief, all present agreed that his entrance into camp was funny indeed. Even the Apache laughed when O hi Cama joked about being welcomed to his own camp by arrows.

Protocol dictated that O hi Cama, politely, defer telling his news to Nanni Chaddi until after the noon meal was finished and they could be momentarily alone. When that time came, O hi Cama wasted no words in telling of the events at the Peralta camp. The look of anger in Nanni Chaddi's eyes was so hot it could start a fire. The young Yavapai stepped back and waited for Nanni Chaddi to speak. He waited for a moment until he saw that his chief had calmed himself and was ready to move forward with what he wished to say to his young subchief.

"O hi Cama, our Apache cousins arrived here last night. They are all subchiefs of their bands. I have told them only briefly what we have in mind to do. They are interested but seem to be waiting for a better reason to join with us than I have given them," said the Yavapai chief. "You have ridden long and hard. Rest yourself until the evening meal. Then I will want you to tell the Apache what you saw yesterday and what it means."

Nanni Chaddi saw the apprehension in O hi Cama's look but said, "You need not be nervous. You speak very well, and you are closer to their age. These Apache look at me with respect, but as they would an old man . . . a grandfather. They will more readily listen to you, O hi Cama."

O hi Cama understood. Even if he had wished to argue the point, he was simply too tired. His wikiup was calling to him. Nanni Chaddi said, "I will have someone wake you in time. Now, rest, O hi Cama."

A small earthquake might not have awakened the exhausted warrior from his well-deserved sleep, so it was not surprising that it took both hands of the rather large Yavapai woman to raise O hi Cama from his rest. For a moment he did not reconcile the wide smile of the woman with where he was or what she wanted. Then, he awakened fully and realized that it was time to return to Nanni Chaddi's wikiup. He spent just a few moments to groom himself, then stepped out into the evening air.

O hi Cama walked slowly but deliberately to Nanni Chaddi's wikiup, where all knew that a council was being held. He was welcomed by all and invited to share the evening meal. They would all speak afterwards. He did his best not to eat too much all at once, but he was so hungry! The Yavapai warrior thought he had shown proper restraint toward overeating, but he had to laugh with the others when one of their guests praised him for his warrior's appetite. When the genial banter died down, Nanni Chaddi rose to speak. "This warrior's appetite is well earned. He has ridden hard to deliver news he has witnessed with his own eyes. But what he has seen is of great importance to all of us. I have spoken of it, but O hi Cama can speak of it in greater detail than I."

"Let O hi Cama speak then of this news," said one of the Apache.

O hi Cama slowly, and with great deliberation, rose to speak. "My brothers, even from the time of the Ancient Ones, our forefathers lived here, and the land was ours. Apache, Navajo, Pima, Yavapai—all belong in this land. Our forefathers conducted themselves with honor. In times of dispute and of conflict, they conducted themselves as men should. They were open to each other, man to man, tribe to tribe. If a war was fought, it was fought without deceit until it was decided to have peace. If one man makes a pact with another, he honors that pact. If one tribe makes a pact with another tribe, it also is honored. From the beginning there have often been wars between our tribes. But the wars were fought, and peace was made, honorably and without deceit."

"Yes. Our forefathers acted as men should," spoke up one of the Apache.

"Then came a time of intruders into this land—land that belongs to all of us. The Spanish came first, then the Mexicans. We all have fought them at various times. Yet they still remained. You, our brothers the Apache, have fought them long and bitterly. You have just been fighting a long war with the Mexicans in what they call Chihuahua. You have done well," O hi Cama continued.

All present murmured words of approval.

"You have driven the Mexicans back into their homes well into Mexico," said O hi Cama.

Again, came murmurs of praise and approval.

"We, the Yavapai, thought we had done the same many years ago," asserted O hi Cama. "Before my life, when Nanni Chaddi was a young man as I am now, Mexicans came here. They made many promises that they would not keep. They deceived our people and tried to enslave them. They came for the yellow stones . . . gold. They cared for nothing but these stones. They scarred Earth Mother to get them. They tore them from her by digging holes in her."

"Yes! We all have seen this before," chimed in the Apache.

"The Yavapai, including the young warrior Nanni Chaddi, rose up and drove them from this land," said O hi Cama to cheers of approval from the Apache.

"Many Yavapai were killed. These Mexicans did not leave easily. Many of them were killed. Yet we drove them away," asserted O hi Cama to loud cheers of praise for Nanni Chaddi and the Yavapai.

"Now the same leader of those Mexicans has returned with many men and weapons to continue tearing the yellow stones from the Earth Mother," said O hi Cama.

Cries of, "No! This cannot be!" arose from the council.

"This leader, Don Miguel Peralta, is older now but has returned. He leads a large force. There are about two hundred miners and fifty Mexican cavalry to protect them, with nearly four hundred mules and horses, mostly mules," continued O hi Cama.

"Ha! We could use those horses and eat the mules," said the Apache, laughing.

"There is more," spoke Nanni Chaddi. "Realizing that much time had passed since this Peralta was here last, I tried to treat the Mexicans with honor. I agreed to allow them to take more yellow stones but only from the holes they had already dug from the last intrusion many years ago. Don Miguel Peralta also promised to place guards around the places of the Ancient Ones to keep his own men from desecrating them. This, I must tell you, he did. But . . ." Nanni Chaddi hesitated then went on. "You tell our brothers more of this, O hi Cama."

"It is hard to believe any of them keeping a promise!" exclaimed one of the Apache.

O hi Cama continued, "Don Miguel had to leave his men here and travel to California, the land that rises by the big water. Before leaving, he put his son Manuel Peralta in command of this force."

"Is he honoring the promises of his father?" questioned the Apache.

"Yesterday afternoon I saw miners laughingly breaking more yellow stones from a new hole in the breast of the Earth Mother," told O hi Cama.

"No! No! No!" shouted the council.

"There is more," said the Yavapai warrior. "On the side of the hill that houses the Ancient Ones, they were digging yet another hole."

"No! They must not disturb the spirits of the Ancient Ones! We must not let this happen!" shouted the Apache subchiefs.

"Drive them out! Kill all of them!" loudly shouted all present. "Kill them now!"

It took many minutes to calm the council. When the entire council had calmed down, O hi Cama said, "Nanni Chaddi remembers the horrors of trying to drive them away the first time. Many died, Yavapai and Mexicans. We all have many reasons to rid our land of these men. Any Mexicans who want the yellow stones must be made to know what will happen to them if they come into our land . . . Yavapai and Apache land! If we are to drive them from all our lands, we must start here. But we cannot just attack them. They are far too many, and most of them are professional soldiers."

"And they have many horses, mules, and weapons for us," reiterated the Apache leaders.

"Yes! All this for all of us, but only if we use our heads," said Nanni Chaddi.

The Apache subchiefs mumbled a moment among themselves. The mumbled discussion over, one stood up and addressed Nanni Chaddi, O hi Cama, and the entire council. "We all want to be a part of this great war that you will make upon the Mexicans. But this is Yavapai land, and you must lead this war. We Apache are great warriors. During this last fight in Chihuahua, we have learned to fight together as one warrior. Our chiefs have together forced the Mexicans to leave much of Apacheria. Tell us what you wish us to do, and we will tell our chiefs. It would surprise all of us if, after those great victories, the Apache would refuse to help you rid your land also of these intruders."

Then O hi Cama rose and faced the Apache, eye to eye. "Which Apache chiefs will you tell of our war?"

The answer was pleasing to the ears of the Yavapai. "Mangas Coloradas, his subchief Cochise, Juh, and Miguel Narbona. When they hear of this sacrilege against the Ancient Ones, this Yavapai war will be an Apache war."

O hi Cama glanced at Nanni Chaddi and was rewarded by a smile of *well done.*

"We have planned for many months how this war might be won," said Nanni Chaddi. "There is a place spoken of by Warrior Woman. Move in closer, my brothers . . ."

27

Manuel Peralta, still smarting from the seeming insubordination of Lieutenant Diego DaVia and Capitán Garces, managed to share a genial breakfast with those two gentlemen. Manuel said, "Gentlemen, I see in the past few days we've managed to be all but packed. When do you think that we should depart?"

"Just as soon as you give the order," replied Capitán Garces.

"And you, Lieutenant?" asked Manuel.

"I think we need to call in our outlying miners today, make final preparations regarding transportation of the gold, and run out of here just as fast as we can," answered Lieutenant DaVia.

Capitán Garces then said, "The weather is not as cool as we'd like, but it is cool enough. I have not checked any inventory of the gold we've collected, but I'd say we might not even be able to carry it all."

"I had hoped to delay our departure until it was cooler, but I suppose we are close enough to end this expedition. Forgive me for my recent behavior. I had become so concerned with command that I overlooked why I was put in command. I hope we have not waited too long," said Manuel Peralta.

At this point, Sergeant Mendoza, huffing and puffing, was seen running toward them along with a very frightened miner. "Capitán, Capitán!" he was shouting.

"What is it, Sergeant? Why the ruckus?" shouted Capitán Garces back at him.

"Yavapai, sir! A party of twenty or so. Way down in the wash under Blue Mountain. They are carrying a white flag and just waiting, sir! The young girl, U Day Ah, is with them. Looks like they want to talk," explained Sergeant Mendoza.

"I'd say so," flatly said Lieutenant DaVia, as if he needed to clarify the issue.

"Sergeant Mendoza, you are in full charge until we return," said Capitán Garces.

Manuel Peralta, Capitán Garces, and Lieutenant DaVia put on their formal attire, mounted their horses, and slowly rode down Camp Creek wash to meet the Yavapai. Lieutenant DaVia, on orders from Capitán Garces, carried the flag of Mexico. The slight morning breeze from the east made the flag unfurl and wave proudly. With the flag of Mexico flying and riding side by side, they were the epitome of Mexican authority.

However, the formation waiting for them in the wash below Blue Mountain looked formidably authoritative also. The Yavapai, dressed in their colorful best, awaited the Mexicans quietly. U Day Ah, with O hi Cama on her right and Nanni Chaddi himself on her left, was slightly ahead of the rest of the Yavapai. These warriors were lined up in a straight line behind the three. All warriors carried knives, bows and arrows, and the short lances so useful in close fighting. All warriors save Nanni Chaddi wore paint.

The Peralta party rode slowly, as if this formal meeting were very important to them. When they were separated by only about ten feet, el capitán commanded, "Halt!" At that point, Manuel Peralta moved slightly forward.

"Nanni Chaddi, Chief of the Yavapai, welcome. It is good to see you again," ventured Manuel Peralta. "I regret that my father, Don Miguel, is not here to greet you."

U Day Ah, who would be interpreter for the entire proceeding, voiced the words of Nanni Chaddi: "I regret that he is not here also. What I have to say should have been spoken to him directly, man to man."

"What would you say to Don Miguel Peralta, Nanni Chaddi?" asked Manuel Peralta.

"I would have said to Don Miguel what I will say to you, his son. You have broken the agreement we made when we first met. You have opened more wounds in the breast of our Earth Mother," said Nanni Chaddi.

"Another vein of the yellow stones was discovered. I felt that to remove it would speed our departure from this land," replied Manuel Peralta. Manuel did not like being challenged on this point, especially when he was dead wrong.

"Your father, Don Miguel, swore this would not be allowed to happen!" argued Nanni Chaddi, his voice beginning to rise in anger.

"There will be no more holes opened in this land," stated Manuel condescendingly. After all, he knew they would be leaving soon anyway.

"No, there will not be any more!" loudly stated Nanni Chaddi. "You have desecrated the hillside of the Ancient Ones. We have seen it! The spirits of our Ancient Ancestors cry for their peace. You have seven days to be gone from this place and the land of the Yavapai. If you are still here, the Yavapai will attack, and you will all be dead!"

"How dare you threaten us! Who the hell do you think you are? You are but a few wandering bands of Yavapai. You just try to attack us! This force of men was designed to fight off any such foolish attack!" shouted Manuel. "Be off with you now! Go back to your rabbit hunting, or whatever you do for entertainment. But remember, if you attack us, you will be dead!"

"I will honor my word. Seven days! No more! I have spoken my last words to you," and, with that, Nanni Chaddi waved his lance in the air, turned, and led his people away at a fast lope.

As the Yavapai delegation loped away, Lieutenant DaVia murmured, "*Hmmmh.* Seven days. Should be quite a party."

"No such thing!" yelled Manuel Peralta. "Business as usual!"

Capitán Garces worriedly spoke up now. "Manuel, he was serious. Did you see the look on the face of O hi Cama? Oh, they were serious all right."

Lieutenant DaVia then said, "Well, what are the orders?"

Capitán said, "Finish packing as soon as you can. We have seven days to get out of here. Let's not waste any of them."

"We'd better call in the outlying miners into the main camp, or we'll begin losing some of them," said Lieutenant DaVia.

"The hell we will!" shouted Manuel Peralta. "I give the orders in this expedition! No painted savage, leader of twenty or thirty desert rabbit hunters, is running me away from these mines. We'll go when I'm damn good and ready to go!"

With that, he brutally turned his horse and raced back, through the main camp, and on to the stone cabin in the canyon. Lieutenant DaVia looked at el capitán and said, "Well, sir. Do we all just go, or maybe shoot him . . . and then go?"

"That is not funny, Lieutenant." retorted el capitán.

"Touch a nerve, Capitán?" asked Lieutenant DaVia. "You were probably thinking the same thing."

"Don't push me, Lieutenant," said el capitán. "We still have our orders."

"Capitán, you have fought Apache many times. So have I. Have you ever seen them pick a fight when they did not have the advantage?" asked Lieutenant DaVia.

"No, I have not," answered el capitán.

"Well, sir, that Nanni Chaddi just gave us the scheduled time of the hostilities," speculated the lieutenant.

"Why?" asked el capitán.

"Because, as I have said before, Nanni Chaddi has only been playing for time. He thinks he'll have enough firepower to do the job sometime after this week," explained Lieutenant DaVia.

"Orders are orders," answered el capitán.

Lieutenant DaVia's frustration was getting to him as el capitán spurred his mount back to camp. The lieutenant chose to walk his mount back to camp. He needed to cool off.

Manuel Peralta kept very much to himself for the next few days. The meeting with the Yavapai had not gone well. He had thought that, when a confrontation did come, he would prevail. Manuel Peralta believed that the size of the Peralta forces and his own presence would be intimidating to these desert-dwelling savages. He had been surprised by the determination of the Yavapai. "Who the hell do they think they are?" he continued to ask himself.

Avoiding Capitán Garces and, especially, Lieutenant DaVia had become a high priority for Manuel. His own anger, plus the nagging thought that they were right, wore heavily upon him. But how dare they question his position! He was Manuel Peralta, son of Don Miguel Peralta, and in complete command of this entire operation. All true, but he was also young and inexperienced in command. He knew it but did not like the thought. He, therefore, issued any necessary orders through Sergeant Mendoza.

The tension in camp among the miners and cavalry both was extremely high. Word had spread concerning the ultimatum given Manuel Peralta by Nanni Chaddi. All believed that an attack would come. Most believed that the Peraltas would overcome the Yavapai. However, all believed that there would be casualties. No one wanted to die by a Yavapai arrow. All kept watchful eyes on the ridges, believing that any attack would begin from there.

— —

The days dragged by. Tempers were running high. Sergeant Mendoza reported to Lieutenant DaVia that, "If all that energy spent fighting with each other was directed toward the Yavapai, we'd have nothing to worry about."

The lieutenant and el capitán had chosen not to intrude on Manuel's self-imposed exile from discussions. Therefore, on the morning of the seventh day after Nanni Chaddi's warning, they were surprised to see Manuel Peralta riding up to their command tent. He dismounted and entered. The two officers rose to greet him.

"Gentlemen, please once again accept my apology for being so discourteous to you both in days past. However, my behavior notwithstanding, nothing has changed concerning my evaluation of our circumstances. Do you understand, gentlemen?" spoke Manuel Peralta.

"Yes, sir!" said both officers.

"Good," continued Manuel. "Yet, in spite of my feelings to the contrary, I do see some wisdom in concentrating our forces for a while. Do you agree that recalling the outlying miners back into the main camp would be wise at this time?"

"Yes, sir!" replied both officers.

"The sooner, the better," added Lieutenant DaVia, in spite of a withering look from Capitán Garces.

"In that case, order a party of your cavalry to go out tomorrow and escort them back within this encampment," said Manuel to el capitán.

"I will lead that mission myself," said Lieutenant DaVia, "and leave right now."

"You will not!" shouted Manuel Peralta. "I will not lead that damn Nanni Chaddi to believe we are too afraid of him to go past his stinking deadline."

"I will leave first thing in the morning," said the lieutenant.

"You will delay until well after the breakfast meal so as not to convey any feeling of urgency, Lieutenant," ordered Manuel. "The Yavapai will be watching us. Do you agree, Capitán?"

"Yes, sir," said el capitán. "They will be watching. However, I agree with Lieutenant DaVia that we should recall the miners as soon as possible."

"You will carry out my orders as given. Questions, gentlemen?" stated Manuel Peralta.

"No questions," was the reply from both men as Manuel departed, although Lieutenant DaVia added under his breath, "Your Majesty."

After Manuel Peralta had left, Capitán Garces ordered, "Lieutenant, you may not be able to leave before morning, but have everything in readiness for a quick departure when you do. You may start your preparations now."

"I already have the men for this patrol all handpicked," said the lieutenant.

Lieutenant DaVia had barely left the tent when Capitán Garces sat down and put his head in his hands. "Why have I so easily relinquished command of my cavalry to this upstart Manuel Peralta? Tomorrow I will more forcefully assert my control over the military portion of this campaign. Yes, it is a campaign. It might as well be a war . . . and probably will be soon."

The thoughts of el capitán focused on the girl, U Day Ah. How he had been starstruck by those eyes. Although many years older than U

Day Ah, he had allowed himself to dream for a while. The dreams had been so pleasant. The beautiful face, the eyes, the full promise of her young curves had made him think of himself in other times. Then the reality of it all was revealed to him, and he had had to face it. Until a few days ago, he would still have dreamed of a life with U Day Ah. Then came the meeting at the foot of Blue Mountain; the look in those eyes spoke volumes to him. The sweet, helpless, young beauty interpreting for Nanni Chaddi could not have been U Day Ah. This woman might just as well have been another Yavapai warrior. She was not only cold, but hard. Could it have been the encounter with Sebriano? Lieutenant DaVia rescued her, but in so doing, had he frightened her by killing him? Does she no longer have any soft feelings for the Peralta expedition . . . for him?

U Day Ah's look had told him all. There was no turning back now. The Yavapai were going to attack, and soon. He must be prepared. El capitán, without telling Manuel Peralta, ordered all firearms prepared for instant warfare. All supplies were to be concentrated, so as to be easily carried by mule back rather than in the wagons. The wagons, if he could get away with it, would be left behind. Capitán Garces believed, whenever the escape began, that it would be a running battle.

Capitán Garces knew and understood that Manuel Peralta had reneged on his original order to accomplish those preparations, but to hell with him! In the upcoming battle—and he firmly now believed it was coming soon—he, Capitán Antonio Garces, would be in command.

28

An hour before breakfast in the main encampment, Manuel Peralta paced slowly around the camp. He had given a direct order that Lieutenant DaVia not leave to recall the outlying miners until after breakfast and, by God, he meant to enforce it. Time passed, but eventually Lieutenant DaVia appeared, walking quite nonchalantly toward the mess table. He passed Manuel without a word. He was determined to make a great show of following Manuel Peralta's order to the full extent of it.

A moment later Capitán Garces addressed Lieutenant DaVia. "Is your detail ready, Lieutenant?"

"Yes, sir!" replied the lieutenant. "As per Manuel Peralta's orders, I will proceed with his orders just as soon after breakfast as I'm damn good and ready, sir."

"Carry on then, Lieutenant, and enjoy your breakfast," said el capitán.

Manuel Peralta, standing some distance away, did manage to overhear the conversation but chose to ignore the blatant slur.

With Manuel standing by . . . an hour later, Lieutenant Diego DaVia, saluting with exaggerated formality, rode out with his handpicked detail of twenty cavalrymen. The plan was to reach each outlying mine in turn, relieve the two soldier guards and miners, and have one of the new cavalrymen escort each group back to the main Peralta encampment.

Unfortunately, the Yavapai also had plans.

The sight that greeted the relief detail as it approached the first mine stiffened each man in the saddle. Hearts stopped, then raced madly as each man thought he, too, might be next. Miners lay before them, scattered all over the clearing, stripped naked, dead of countless arrow wounds. The arrows, evidently in order to conserve them for future use, had been pulled out and removed from the bodies of their victims. The detail of cavalrymen had to fight off nausea as they surveyed the horrid scene before them.

Lieutenant DaVia recovered and ordered the men forward at a gallop to the next mine. Horribly, the previous scene was repeated, and repeated, and repeated!

It was late in the evening when the detail returned to the Peralta camp. Campfires were burning, as if to convince the Yavapai of the strength of the Peralta expedition. Lieutenant DaVia rode in at the head of the procession. Upon arriving at the tent of el capitán, he fired his pistol—once. Capitán Garces rushed out, pistol in hand. The look on Lieutenant DaVia's face told him all that he needed to know. They were dead! Miners, soldiers—all were dead!

El capitán leaped on his horse and, dismissing the men, raced to the Peralta cabin. As he raced off, he yelled, "Diego, you stay where you are!" He did not want Diego DaVia killing Manuel Peralta tonight.

Manuel Peralta had heard the shot fired by Lieutenant DaVia and was waiting as el capitán rode up the canyon to the cabin. El capitán's plunging horse nearly trampled Manuel Peralta as el capitán halted him and dismounted nearly on top of him. Manuel nearly fell backwards as el capitán charged him. "What the hell!?" Manuel screamed.

"They are dead! They are all dead! Every miner at every outlying mine! Seventy-five miners . . . dead! Fifteen cavalrymen . . . dead!" screamed el capitán at Manuel Peralta.

Manuel hardly took a breath before yelling, "The damned savage liars! They did not wait until after the seventh day! Damn them!"

"They did this all today. They did not lie. They were about an hour ahead of DaVia all day, with different war parties. We heard nothing. It was done in silence, with arrows," related el capitán.

Manuel stood, stammering, unable to form any words of any kind. How could he? After all, Nanni Chaddi had given him an ultimatum, honorably, and then acted upon it as promised. He, Manuel Peralta, had treated the Yavapai's words as without merit. The war had started, and he, Manuel, had no idea how to handle it.

Capitán Garces knew how to handle it. He stepped forward within an inch of Manuel Peralta's face. In words spoken in a tone raspy, low, and fraught with menace, Capitán Garces said, "Manuel Peralta, you are no longer in command of this expedition. It is my responsibility to protect this expedition. I have been lax in that responsibility, deferring to your command. That is over now. I am forced to assume command. Any objections by you will see you placed in chains, to be released only when we must fight for our lives. Starting immediately, you will take orders from me!"

"The gold stored in this camp is mine! You will not rob me of it!" screamed Manuel.

"What is left of the men in this expedition is my priority now. If we can escape with the gold, we will. We will meet at my tent one hour before dawn," ordered el capitán.

———

Why everyone waited until dawn no one knows. It was not as if anyone in that camp could sleep that night. Yet, one hour before dawn, Manuel Peralta approached the command tent of Capitán Garces. Upon entering, all inside were silent. Manuel Peralta, son of Don Miguel Peralta, said simply, "I was wrong, horribly wrong. My poor decision has cost the lives of many men. I will never be able to forget it. Capitán Garces, I will follow your orders. You are in full command to get us all home."

"Thank you, Manuel," said el capitán. "I will add that I have not forgotten our original mission to bring home as much gold as possible. To that end I will hear any ideas. But remember, we have little, if any, time."

Lieutenant DaVia's look showed his thoughts. He wanted to take as little gold as possible and hightail it out of there.

Manuel offered his idea. "Each man will pack one saddlebag with gold, about fifty pounds each man. Each mule should be packed with two bags of gold, about one hundred pounds. Wagons . . ."

"No wagons!" interrupted Lieutenant DaVia.

"Then all extra gold will remain in the warehouse cabin. Hopefully, someday it can be retrieved," said Manuel.

"Do we dare waste any time trying to store this gold?" asked Lieutenant DaVia.

El capitán replied, "I do not believe that the Yavapai will attack today. It would be too soon. If they were at full strength, they would have struck en masse yesterday. They will stand down to assess whether they've made their point yesterday, watching to see if we leave, or they are waiting for reinforcements from somewhere. Either way, we should have some time. But we need to get at it."

"Stashing that gold in the cabin is asking for it to disappear," said Lieutenant DaVia. "Put it in the lower shaft, the horizontal shaft of that mine right behind the cabin. The Yavapai will not want to enter the darkness of that mine. After the gold is stashed, we will pile rocks in the entrance in order to hide it. Put brush in front of it and hope for the best. But I really don't give a damn about that gold. Let's just get the hell out of here!"

All were in agreement. Lieutenant DaVia wanted the men to only pack as much gold as they could carry and still ride fast. The actual amount would be left to the officers loading the horses and mules. Many mules had already been lost at the outlying mines and that gold scattered. All knew that this expedition was not going to bring home nearly as much gold as promised.

The work started immediately. No one showed any laziness that day. Fear is quite a motivator. Everyone thought that the Yavapai were watching. No one really cared, though. The work took but a few days. But they finished their assignments and were ready to run. Now they rested. The next day would come soon enough.

———

Manuel Peralta slept little over the days of preparation to leave. He knew he had failed in his promise to his father, Don Miguel. However, he firmly believed that he could get the miners and soldiers safely home to Sonora, with as much gold as could be salvaged. Sooner or later an expedition could return to retrieve the remainder. That thought was all that had kept him going over the course of those few very difficult days.

———

The evening before the planned departure, Manuel had his dinner with el capitán and Lieutenant DaVia in the command tent. It had been his plan that departure would occur at dawn the next day. "Is all in readiness for tomorrow at dawn?" asked Manuel.

"Dawn will find us three or four hours already on our way," calmly replied Lieutenant DaVia.

"Leaving just after midnight! Why?" asked Manuel.

"Lieutenant DaVia's idea," said el capitán. "And I think he is right. Think about it. We are armed with muskets, cap and ball pistols. It takes both hands to load and fire. In the heat of battle, it is time consuming. Lieutenant DaVia and I agree that, once we are underway, any fight will actually be a running battle on mule or horseback. It will be difficult to use these weapons effectively, if at all, on the run."

"The Yavapai, whether lying in wait for us in ambush, or riding, can shoot arrows faster and probably more accurately," added the lieutenant. "If the Yavapai are serious about finishing us off, and I believe they are, they probably will not expect us to leave the confines of this wash in the middle of the night."

"I am hopeful that we can make it to Needle Rocks at the Rio Verde before they can overtake us," said el capitán.

"In other words, we can expect to fight as we run at least from Needle Rocks forward," stated Manuel. "We will lose many men and animals in that kind of battle."

"Speed will be our only weapon," said the lieutenant, matter-of-factly.

"Beyond that, I do not know," said el capitán. "We will be running and hoping for luck."

Manuel Peralta voiced an idea that had been on his mind for some time. "You are telling me that our firepower is really no good to us unless we can fortify ourselves somewhere. Am I right?"

"It boils down to that," said el capitán.

"Capitán, you of course remember the box canyon where we halted for a few days coming here?" said Manuel.

"I do," said el capitán. "I remember the canyon that lies on the northwest point of Sierra de la Espuma, Superstition Mountain. Am I correct?"

"If we can make it to that box canyon, we could hold them off indefinitely. After all, they really cannot have an entire army against us," said Manuel.

"What do you think, Lieutenant?" asked el capitán.

"I think that *if* we get out of here with most of our animals and men, and *if* we survive a running battle all the way to the Rio Salado, and *if* we can make it to that box canyon, then we'd damn sure better have our own men positioned on the ridges that make that canyon a box," answered Lieutenant DaVia. "If we are up against more Yavapai, or even Apache, than we think, they might have enough men to command those heights. That, gentlemen, would ruin our whole day."

"I do not see much choice," agreed el capitán. "Lieutenant DaVia, has Sergeant Mendoza been given the order to wrap any object that will make a noise as we leave?"

"Yes, Capitán," said Lieutenant DaVia. "He guarantees that there will be no clanks or rattles as we sneak out of here."

"In that case, gentlemen, get some rest. I know better than to expect sleep, but do the best you can," said El Capitán Garces.

29

El capitán was right. There was no sleep for anyone. At approximately one o'clock in the morning, el capitán quietly gave the order for the procession to move out. Lieutenant DaVia's idea to leave in the dark of night evidently did catch the Yavapai by surprise. The caravan left the encampment, moving not immediately down the Camp Creek wash, but veering south around a wash that paralleled Camp Creek called Blue Wash. About a mile later, the Peraltas turned eastward to reenter Camp Creek wash, well below the rough country immediately southeast of the former encampment. Now they were able to make better time.

The sun had just made its appearance on the eastern horizon, blinding the men and horses of the Peralta expedition as they made their way through the switchbacks of the canyon nearing Needle Rocks.

El capitán had hoped to be able to rest a bit and water the livestock and men at Needle Rocks, but about a mile northwest of that point, the Yavapai began their attack. Loud war cries accompanied a shower of arrows as the Peraltas made their way through the switch-backing canyon. Men, mules, and horses began their run through the canyon . . . but not all of them. Arrows fired in the dawn glare and shadowy darkness behind the last of the switchbacks randomly claimed an untold number of victims. The remaining column of men barely heard the screams of the left-behind wounded men and animals as they, themselves, now raced for their lives down the canyon.

The hoped-for rest at Needle Rocks was now impossible, as the column of miners and cavalry plunged their mounts into the Rio Verde, trying to

Needle Rocks

use the easier terrain on the east side of the river. The hail of Yavapai arrows continued, as did the terrifying war cries. Some of those arrows accounted for more casualties among the Peralta men and animals. The Yavapai were firing their barrage with impunity from behind the thick desert foliage. The Peraltas, for the most part, were never able to see their attackers, much less return their fire. At this point, the Peralta leaders had no idea just how many casualties they had suffered. The run continued with as much speed as they could muster through high weeds and low scrub brush.

El capitán had taken the lead, concentrating what was left of his cavalry at the forefront of the column in the hope that they would be able to clear any resistance to their flight. Manuel Peralta took the right flank to keep the column intact as they galloped for their lives. Sergeant Mendoza and Private Muñoz were on the left of the fleeing column to stabilize that side. Lieutenant DaVia took it upon himself to ride at the rear of the column. From there he could act as a whip, not allowing any stragglers.

From his position at the front of the fleeing column of miners and cavalry, el capitán could not concentrate on anything except leading his men through any route that seemed the path of least resistance. That was a futile effort. The reality was that the column simply crashed through any and all obstacles. This was difficult enough, but he soon began to realize that he had no concept at all of what was happening behind him. He had no choice but to plunge onward as best he could.

Manuel Peralta found himself in a similar situation. He had no choice but to keep the right side of the column racing forward as fast as they could. However, he found himself often riding through a hail of arrows. The war cries of the Yavapai, in addition to their being terrifying, were seemingly incessant. He was aware of men and mules and horses falling from the merciless Yavapai arrows. In spite of his fear, Manuel Peralta would have stopped to render aid if he could. But he couldn't. He had no choice but to yell out words of encouragement to his men and race on.

Sergeant Mendoza and Private Muñoz found themselves in the same predicament, helpless to do anything but ride hard while dodging arrows. But even as they fled with the entire column, in spite of the screaming fear that controlled them, they wondered: where the hell did the Yavapai get so many warriors? This was no small band of rabbit-chasing desert savages.

Lieutenant DaVia was aware of all that was happening. He was facing the arrows. The horror of wounded men and livestock, screaming in pain and terror as they fell and were left behind to the merciless Yavapai, tore at his very soul. There was no chance at all for the cavalry—much less the miners—to retaliate in any way. He also was seeing that the Yavapai were attacking in greater numbers than Manuel and el capitán had imagined. All he could see was the result. He knew it! Lieutenant DaVia realized that this was not just a run and shoot action on the part of the Yavapai but part of a grander plan to wipe out the whole Mexican expedition. He did not yet understand how it would work, but he could see it unfolding. He had been right. "Damn! There has to be a way out of this!"

But the race was still on. And it continued with very few opportunities of any kind to rest. There were occasional sandbars in the Rio Verde. Thanks to the wide-open space provided by the wide sandy shoals, the column was able to regroup and collectively catch its breath for a few minutes at each. At least the horses and mules could catch their breath and drink some of the now-muddied water. The Yavapai seemed hesitant to try a frontal assault out in the open sandbar area.

Rio Verde sand bar

Then the Yavapai, and their heretofore unknown allies, managed to get too close, and the Peralta party had to resume the desperate race for their lives. But the horses and mules involved in this race were suffering greatly. Many had been wounded or killed. The survivors were exhausted beyond belief. Plus, they were loaded down by packs filled with gold.

The day wore on, with more and more casualties. The Peraltas took advantage of every opportunity to use the sandbars to rest. Many horses, mules, and men were gone. Each man had paid a terrible price for joining the expedition. There were no survivors among those men who had fallen along the miles; those men were dead. Mules were wounded, dead, or taken by the Yavapai. The gold, the reason for this ill-fated adventure, was already being scattered in the desert rocks. And all day long the sun shone white hot, unmercifully on the embattled miners and cavalry.

The exhausted men and animals reached the point where the Rio Verde flowed into the Rio Salado. El capitán, without any hesitation, led the column into the water at breakneck speed and across to the south bank of the Rio Salado. The arrow barrages stopped. The continuous ambushes ceased. Was it because the sun was moving low in the west? Was the onslaught over? The Peraltas did not know. So far, none of the Peralta expedition could say he had killed an enemy. But the unseen enemy had bloodied them.

El capitán was glad to see Manuel Peralta still mounted on his nearly played-out horse. Lieutenant DaVia slowly walked his heavily breathing horse toward the others. "We have lost possibly half of our whole expedition," said el capitán in a low voice. A low whisper was all the voice he could muster at the moment. "Has anyone seen Sergeant Mendoza or Private Muñoz? They had been positioned on the left flank of the column."

Manuel said, "I lost sight of them way back upriver."

Lieutenant DaVia reported, "I saw Private Muñoz as I passed him just south of Needle Rocks. He was dead with an arrow through his throat. Sergeant Mendoza was luckier. His horse was killed by arrows and went down. The sergeant died instantly when he hit the ground."

"I had so hoped that fine old man would make it," said el capitán.

"Have they called it quits for tonight? Maybe they have done all they planned to do," offered Manuel.

El capitán started to say, "Maybe so. We have not seen them for a little—"

"We'll see those devils soon enough," interrupted the lieutenant. "This is all part of some plan of theirs. I saw it developing while riding in the back of this so-called column."

"What the hell do you mean by that, Lieutenant?" demanded el capitán.

"Think about it! At no time did those bastards ever show themselves. There is no possible way for those ambushers to ride with us and keep shooting like they did the whole damn way. We had the least trouble-some terrain. Those Yavapai have reinforcements and plenty of them," expanded Lieutenant DaVia.

"So? We expected that," stated Manuel.

El capitán ventured his opinion: "It doesn't seem like much of a plan to me—just shoot at us as we run by."

"Damned effective though," sneered Manuel Peralta.

"Wake up, children! These devils were already in place. Damn it! They knew where we would be, and they were waiting!" the lieutenant shouted. "Damn it! We are being herded someplace!"

Manuel said, "They can't have any more warriors than we have had to deal with already today."

"What they had has killed about half of the men that started this day. Killing some of them would help. We did not do any of that today. I'd say they had more than enough warriors to do the job," reiterated Lieutenant DaVia. "And think about this: they are not just staying back where they were along the Rio Verde. They are going to visit us again!"

"So, what do we do now?" asked Manuel Peralta.

El capitán, albeit shaken by this day's fiasco, still maintained his command. He said, "We'll allow what is left of our forces to eat some cold food . . . no fires. Then we continue our march."

"To where?" asked Manuel Peralta.

"I'm not sure," replied el capitán, clearly shaken by the day's disaster.

Lieutenant DaVia submitted his idea. "During the dark of night, we must move east . . . toward that Superstition Mountain. We must march through a pass between low mountains to the north and to the south. Once through that pass we must make a choice: make a run for it to the shelter of that box canyon and fort up, or, turn due south and run directly to the Rio Gila and on to Sonora."

"On what do we base that decision?" asked Manuel Peralta.

"I think I understand what you are saying, Lieutenant," said el capitán. "Did anyone else notice that, in spite of the fact that they must have captured many of our muskets and pistols, no shots, only arrows, were fired by the Yavapai? They must not know how to use the guns."

Lieutenant DaVia further explained: "If we are being chased only by the Yavapai, then this battle may be over. If so, we can break south to Sonora. If we face actual musket fire, then we also are facing the Apache. They know how to fire those weapons."

Manuel Peralta got the idea. "If we are fired upon by muskets, we must turn into the box canyon to fight them off." The three men traded looks of agreement.

"Twenty minutes. Then we move out," said el capitán.

30

The men, as exhausted as they were, moved out quietly in column to the east. In spite of the day's horror, the men moved out. They were too frightened to do otherwise. There was only starlight to see by. No moonlight to give away their position. They marched in silence, each man wrapped in his own thoughts stunned by the horror of what had happened to them that day. Each man prayed that with daylight no sign would be seen of the Yavapai. They marched on leading what gold-laden mules and horses had managed to survive the day's barrage of arrows. El capitán and Manuel Peralta rode at the forefront of the column. Lieutenant DaVia once again rode at the rear to prevent stragglers, for to be a straggler was certain death.

The dark night wore on.

At the first hint of gray light that precedes the dawn, the Peralta column, now consisting of approximately eighty men, arrived at the decision point. The low mountains to the immediate north and to the south had just given way to open desert. The immense dark form of Superstition Mountain loomed ahead. A few miles to the northeast, the box canyon awaited them. To the south of the column, west of Superstition, lay the open desert that had brought them north from Sonora. El Capitán Garces halted the column and ordered the men to rest for a while.

Lieutenant DaVia joined the two others in command. "Well, here we are. What do you both think we should do?"

"From what I can see, and that is not much, we are alone here," said Manuel Peralta. "Maybe we can just turn south to Sonora."

El Capitán Garces advised caution. "Let us not move too soon. If attacked in force out there in the open desert, in our present condition, we won't stand much of a chance."

"How long must we wait to be sure?" asked Manuel.

"I do not think I will ever be sure. But whatever direction we take, I'll need more light to do it," snapped el capitán.

The column rested another fifteen minutes or so. The light had improved enough so that the men could see some distance into the desert. If there was anything out there, it was not moving. Lieutenant DaVia said, "Gentlemen, we must move in one direction or another and soon. There will soon be enough light to see everything, and we will stick out in this openness like a sore thumb."

"I've never considered myself a coward. But I have a very bad feeling about making a run through that open desert. I do not see them, but I feel them out there. Just waiting," voiced Capitán Garces.

"My father used that box canyon previously with success. I say we rush to it. If we must fight, we can do it from there. If not, we can lick our wounds and then proceed home to Sonora," offered Manuel Peralta.

"We know not what sanctuary we can find out in that open desert," voiced el capitán. "I say we head for the box canyon."

"Voting is over. Let's move," said the lieutenant.

The column moved out slightly northeast toward the canyon they hoped would provide a natural fortress as well as water. The men marched, leading their gold-laden horses and mules toward the expected sanctuary. The sun still hid below the eastern horizon. They had moved about five miles toward their goal when the roar of musket fire shattered the silence. Apache! Gunfire from the south side of the column. Within seconds a half-dozen men went down. The men in the column did not need to wait for the order to run for the canyon. The slight rest, plus mortal fear, provided just enough energy to send them galloping forward at breakneck speed.

Lieutenant DaVia whipped his horse frantically while yelling, "Damn, damn, damn! Apache! Damn it! I knew it. Damn Nanni Chaddi! And damn that woman!"

The screams of the wounded animals added to the men's terror as they raced for that canyon. They could see it now.

View west from Massacre Ground

The entrance seemed very wide. They remembered entering it before to regroup and repair on their trip northward. They raced toward it as if it alone could give them new life. Each man now prayed to whatever god he held in his heart for one more chance at life. That life was never more in danger now that the Apache had, without doubt, entered the fight.

The undergrowth tore at them all as they charged through it. El capitán and Manuel Peralta led the panic-stricken group of men through prickly pear cactus, thorny ocotillo, scrub ironwood, and saguaro past the wide-open entrance deeper into the box canyon. Lieutenant DaVia, riding at the rear of the column, was witness to more casualties as they dropped to enemy fire. Approximately fifteen more men fell to Apache gunfire as they raced into the canyon. The lieutenant became aware that his worst fears were well-founded. Gunfire was coming at them now from both sides, from north and south, as the column plummeted forward. They were being herded into that canyon.

He screamed, "Capitán! Capitán! Turn and fight now! They are waiting for us!" But to no avail. He could not be heard. He had no choice but to ride into that perceived trap and fight alongside his compadres.

Apache gunfire was raining on them from both sides. Mounted Yavapai and Apache were attacking en masse from the rear as the Peraltas continued their wild retreat deeper into the canyon. The canyon walls became steep and rocky. Unyielding rocky walls to the right were populated with more Apache than the lieutenant could estimate under the current conditions. The walls on the left, pockmarked by gaping holes where large boulders had once been lodged, were defended by Apache, standing shoulder to shoulder, high on the crest of the canyon wall.

Massacre Ground

In spite of the withering gunfire, many of the Peraltas made it through the hail of lead, following El Capitán Garces and Manuel Peralta up the fifty-foot slope at the back of the canyon. The rising morning sun just clearing the edge of the eastern slope blinded the Mexicans struggling so hard to reach the summit of that slope. Lieutenant DaVia, charging along the left side as close to the wall as possible, was able to witness the others charge up the east slope. His eyes beheld the spectacle as Capitán Garces and Manuel Peralta neared the top. In that blinding sunlight, the entire length of that back wall—the east wall—became a solid mass of Apache warriors. The warriors charged into the exhausted, fleeing miners and cavalrymen. Lances and war clubs, due to the close-in fighting, were the only weapons used by the attackers. The result was deadly. War clubs and lances used with deadly skill, by energized Yavapai and Apache warriors, against exhausted miners and cavalry; the Peraltas never had a chance. All were dead, including Capitán Garces and Manuel Peralta, in less than five minutes.

Lieutenant DaVia had become a part of a plunging, wild-eyed mass of riderless horses and mules, dust, gunfire, and a sky darkened by arrows. The lieutenant's horse struck, nearly simultaneously by numerous arrows, reared backwards. The falling animal threw Lieutenant DaVia against the pockmarked north wall of the canyon. He fell back into one of the low, gaping holes in the base of the wall, his now-dead horse blocking the hole from sight. The backward fall, plus a solid blow from striking the wall, rendered him, mercifully, unconscious.

"Pock holes"

The nightmare of what had happened to him over the past forty-eight hours played over and over in the unconscious mind of Lieutenant Diego DaVia. He was unaware of his writhing in agony as images of the slaughter of his comrades in arms continuously plagued his pain-wracked mind.

Jolted from unconsciousness, he awakened. He knew not what had awakened him. Perhaps the pain in his head; perhaps the overpowering smell of dead men and animals alike; or perhaps it was the deafening silence in place of that incredible din as he had left consciousness. He lay there, smashed back in a hole in the canyon wall partly covered by the dirt and small stones that fell on him when he struck the wall. The dead body of his horse lay in front and partially upon him. The Apache and Yavapai had evidently overlooked him because of this.

Lieutenant DaVia waited patiently for several minutes before even trying to move. He had no way of knowing whether he had been in that hole for a few hours or several days. He waited for any sound, any shadow that would indicate that the Apache and Yavapai were still about. After what seemed an eternity and sensing nothing moving, he tried to get a better view of his surroundings. What he saw looking from behind his dead horse's neck made him reach for his neck bandana to tie around his nose and mouth to lessen the nausea. The late evening sun bathed the whole slope of the box canyon in what would normally be a beautiful orange hue. That evening, the hue just accentuated the horror of it all.

After much effort, the lieutenant freed himself from under the neck and shoulders of his horse and crept out into the open. The sight was revolting. The dead were everywhere: in the cactus, in underbrush of every sort, draped over the numerous rock formations that had made for a beautiful scene the previous visit, but that evening added a macabre aspect to the entire canyon.

The dead and already bloating bodies of the men had been stripped of everything the Apache and Yavapai thought to be useful to them. Wounded horses and mules had been killed and left where they had fallen. Many horses and mules were simply gone. The horses were to be used by their new owners; the mules were to be eaten. The bodies of the men had been mutilated . . . hopefully after they were already dead. Lieutenant DaVia forced the alternative out of his mind. The image of that alternative was just too horrible to contemplate.

He soon found the bodies of Capitán Garces and Manuel Peralta lying near each other, their swords and other weapons, not surprisingly, missing. However, it looked as though they had fought to the bitter end. There was evidence that dead warriors near them had been carried away by their fellow warriors. The only others in that canyon were dead Mexicans and one very much alive Lieutenant Diego DaVia.

DaVia's only thought at this point was to "get the hell out of this place!" But he needed food and water. Everything had been stripped from horses and mules and men by the warriors as their plunder. DaVia's water canteen and supply of jerky were still under his own dead horse. It took some time and a huge amount of work to dig under the horse to retrieve it, but he did it.

The horses and mules taken by the warriors had been outfitted with packs containing the Peraltas' precious gold. Probably very few of the warriors realized the potential value of that gold in future trading with Mexicans or anyone else. It was discarded in crevices or in the Rio Salado and disappeared, in most cases, forever. Some of it became float gold left in that stark canyon. But, either unseen by the warriors or thought not to be worth any effort to retrieve, were the saddlebags of Lieutenant Diego DaVia.

Once past his initial revulsion, DaVia had collected his canteen and weapon from under his horse and was about ready to begin his journey away from the scene of carnage. Then, having regained his faculties, he had dug the saddlebag filled with gold from the torn and broken saddle. He did not want to forget that! All this had nearly drained him of physical strength, but his instinct to survive forced him onward.

Unknown to Diego DaVia, two mounted warriors, unseen from their vantage point near Green Rock on the western slope of Superstition Mountain, noted his survival and his walk from the massacre grounds. They marveled that he had survived that brutal onslaught. They were themselves brave warriors, but both were in awe at the strong medicine of this man who walked away from the dead. Each would tell of him to their fellow warriors. He would be known as "Dead Man Who Walks Away" and, by those who had heard of him, be allowed to go in peace because of what he had done and because of their fear of his powerful medicine.

As "Dead Man Who Walks Away" disappeared into the dusk, the young shaman of the Apache and O hi Cama, warrior of the Yavapai, rode off in different directions to their own people, each to tell of what he had seen and hoped never again to see: "Dead Man Who Walks Away." O hi Cama had recognized, even from the distance, the soldier whom he respected as a fellow warrior—Lieutenant Diego DaVia. He would be sure to honor him by telling of his identity and his powerful medicine throughout the tribes and, thus, secure him safe passage.

Dead Man Who Walks Away – Part II: The Survivor / The Dutchman's Gold completes the legend of the origin of the gold of the Lost Dutchman Mine.

About the Author

Herbert Dean Ely, educated primarily in Illinois and East Tennessee, spent time with the U.S. Air Force, which included being stationed within the Strategic Air Command—Underground. After the military, he served in management and executive positions in both the cement and the armored car/ATM industries.

He has resided for the past forty years in Arizona near Superstition Mountain. This has resulted in a keen interest in the legends of the Southwest, including the Lost Dutchman Mine and the Peralta Massacre. He was certainly not the first, but was one of the very few who have located and visited the Lost Dutchman Mine.

www.ingramcontent.com/pod-product-compliance
Lightning Source LLC
Chambersburg PA
CBHW032120020726
47494CB00007BA/2156